Levi

A BOY'S SEARCH FOR A DADDY'S LOVE

TED VICK

INFIX PUBLISHING

infix@infix.mgacoxmail.com

Ted Vick/ Infix Publishing
infix@infix.mgacoxmail.com

Publisher's Note: This is a work of fiction. Names, characters, places, and incidents are a product of the author's imagination. Locales and public names are sometimes used for atmospheric purposes. Any resemblance to actual people, living or dead, or to businesses, companies, events, institutions, or locales is completely coincidental.

Ordering Information:
Quantity sales. Special discounts are available on quantity purchases by corporations, associations, and others. For details, contact the "Special Sales Department" at the address above.

Levi/Ted Vick -- 1st ed.
ISBN: 978-1-7330715-1-2

Table of Contents

To my wonderful wife, Betty.

The love of my life.

CHAPTER 1

*N*othing was the same then, in the fifties, not a man, not a woman, not a white, not a black. Alex lived during that time, with his father and mother, one younger sister and two older brothers. He was the one stuck in the middle, not himself, not someone else, the same as being nothing.

His family name was Morgan, it was written in dripping paint on a mailbox, rusted and dented, with a door that did not close. There were other names, the same as his last, on at least a dozen mailboxes, some close and others far away. That is, as far away as a small community would allow.

The Morgan's were mixed in blood with the Cherokee. Most of them were farmers. And like their ancestors, they wanted to be left alone, alone to till the land, to plant and to harvest.

It had the promise of a better day, for one such family, that day in August 1956. Alex ran to the truck where his daddy, Robert, was waiting. He was quiet as he climbed into the cab. It had been a long time since either one of them felt any need to speak, much less carry on a conversation.

The slam of the door, and the fall of ash on a shirt of plaid, Alex had seen it a hundred times or more. With the brush of the hand, his daddy sent it drifting past his khaki pants and onto the floor. It was coated now, this floor turned gray, just like yesterday and the day before.

Robert's hand trembled as he jerked the gearshift of the pickup, a 1949 Studebaker. They pulled out of the yard and onto a road of red clay. Alex leaned toward the open window to feel the coolness of the wind against his face. He closed his eyes for a moment. His dreams of distant places were cut short by the sound of his daddy's voice.

"Going to miss me next week?"

Waiting for Alex to answer, he sucked the last draw from his cigarette, before tossing it out the window.

"What about Buster?" Alex said.

"He can take care of himself, Buster has been chasing cars for years, he ain't hurt yet."

There was nothing else Alex wanted to say. He turned again, toward the window, away from his daddy's stare. In a few minutes, they were in front of Sallie Mays' house. The family had gathered on the porch, waiting to start a new day in the same old way.

The house was nothing more than a shack in the middle of a weed patch. It squatted there, low to the ground, with no beauty to see. Not a square piece of wood in sight, not in the front, nor along its side. A roof of tar paper in one place and rusty strips of tin in another.

The front door, as well as the window panels, were gray, faded old and cracked. They all sagged alike as if in agreement to escape, from this heat, cold, and sad talk.

A spring garden lay next to the house. It was dead now, covered in a blanket of brown grass and sandspurs. The only clean spots around the house were between the porch and the road. Behind the house was a crooked pig trail of a path leading to the outhouse.

Alex was glad he lived in a six-room house, with a front door view of the backyard. Some people called it a shotgun house, with rooms, three to the side. Also, he had decent clothes to wear. Being without shoes was his choice. They had a yard of grass and no reason to pick cotton.

It seemed odd that these people on the porch were just like them, like Alex, with a face both happy and empty at the same time. They were all kin to each other in some way or another, this family that included the grandma and a baby boy, a boy nicknamed, 'June Bug'. He was too young to pick cotton but old enough to tag along.

The last time they were there, Robert asked Sallie May if June Bug belonged to her.

"No, sir, he ain't none of mine. The hurricane we had a few years back, blew him here, all the way from Florida. That storm came stomping and a knocking at my door in the middle of the night.

"I found him there, dumped on my front porch, with no more care than a sack of potatoes. I started not to bring him inside. I thought he might be washed away by morning.

"Storms bring bad luck. Mama said I did the right thing. She kinda laid claim to him. He makes me nervous the way he runs about, he won't be still, not for a minute."

She seemed to enjoy telling that story, Alex tried to figure out how much of it was true.

His favorite person was the grandma. Her name was Ester. She could pick three hundred pounds of cotton in a day. No one else in the family could come close to that amount.

Her dress was without any bright colors, somewhat ragged and loose-fitting, except for the part that draped over the slump of her shoulders. She had shoes, just no socks. There was not a slow bone in her body as she grabbed a spot on the tailgate. If she had any aches and pains, it did not show, nor, did she complain.

"Get them picking sacks and come on," she said to the teenage girls on the porch.

"Don't give me that look, I might be old, but I can still put a whipping on you."

They threw the sacks into the truck, and joined the others for the trip down the washboard road, and later, the hedgerow lane. There was little talk among them, with no excitement to speak of. Not to say, they were without laughter, only that, it was short-lived.

Ester was the first one off the truck.

"Y'all come on, you act like you never seen a cotton patch before."

The grass and weeds, wet with dew, did not slow Ester down, she hurried to claim her row. She had the body of a worker, skin the texture of leather, her face stern.

The town crew was late. It was not a good sign. By the time they showed up, the local help was already in the field. The boss of the group moved slow. Slow to get out of his truck, slow to say he was sorry.

"You do realize what time it is?" Robert said.

"You know how young people are, you can't get them out of bed."

"Maybe I made a mistake, can they pick cotton?"

"Yes, sir. I will make sure they do."

"If you want the extra penny a pound, you better."

"Alex, I'm going back to the house, keep a watch on the town people. If anything goes wrong, let me know."

Alex spent most of his time talking to June Bug. He was a sight that morning, singing a song his grandmother had taught him. Toes in the dirt, a grin on his face, clapping with a beat.

First time I saw the boll weevil
He was a-sitting' on the square
Next time I saw him
He had his whole family there.

It was no laughing matter for the Morgans. In 1915, the boll weevil came to Georgia, spotted for the first time in Thomas County. The weevil ruined part of the crop by eating and laying eggs inside the boll, also known as the white flower.

By 1919 Savannah was no longer the hub of 'King Cotton.' Georgia never recovered from the damage. However, for the Morgan's, it remained a better crop than most.

Alex noticed Ester among the short stalks of cotton. She moved fast, with both hands, her fingertips cut too often as she pulled the white lint from its bur. And then, with the same speed, never slowing, she stuffed the cotton into her sack. It was a homemade croaker sack, a good ten foot long. The straps cut into her shoulder as she pulled it through the dirt.

Except for lunch, unlike the younger folk, she seldom stopped to rest.

By noon the temperature reached ninety, and above. The mason jars of water that sat in the shade of the hedgerow were now without any coolness. However, the wetness felt good against parched lips and dry throat.

Alex hated the smell of the sardines that some brought for lunch. A few had crackers and a slice of rat-trap cheese. Going back to the field to work, or going to the bathroom with no trees around, he did not know which they dreaded the most.

The talk found among them during early morning hours, faded into the silence of the afternoon heat. With nothing else to say, they scattered throughout the field. Alex wondered what they were thinking, or if they thought anything at all. When all the standing and bending became too painful, they continued down the row of cotton stalks on bent knees.

By late afternoon, the town people had already quit. Later, the sound of the truck horn echoed over the landscape of unpicked cotton. Alex's brothers, Frank and Norman had arrived with the truck, a two-ton truck, Army surplus with faded green paint.

The local help and the town people said nothing, not to one another. Ester called them brown-skinned and lazy, just smart mouth kids, too stupid to know their place. Later, the low talk among her family turned into plain-spoken words.

Ester went up to Frank and pointed toward the town people, "They got trash in the cotton."

They noticed the gesture and Frank walking toward them.

"You know what she is talking about, don't you?"

"She needs to mind her own business. We ain't emptying no sacks."

"You will if you want to get paid."

Frank enjoyed bossing people around. He was like his daddy. They both treated black people the same.

"Ester, you all get to the weigh-up scale. Norman, go help daddy. I'm going to stay and make sure they get all the trash out, can't trust these people."

Frank was like that, he saw no need to talk behind anyone's back. What were they going to do about it? Robert was close by, watching, and waiting.

The scale, with its hook, dangled from the center of an oak pole. Frank placed one end of the timber on his shoulder, Norman did the same. Both tried not to wobble as the heavy sacks cleared the ground.

Robert moved the pea along the bar, an iron arm with etched numbers below and notches above. With a quick guess, he dropped the pea into a groove, and then a slower moving and dropping. Hoping for another pound, no one looked away until the bar came to a stop.

They worked all day, for that moment, the money already spent. A hundred pounds, sometimes two or more. At the end of the day, the results never changed. They didn't say it out loud, yet there were whispers of discontent concerning the final weight. Robert paid them off with dollar bills, and some change, no one said thank you, not Robert, not anyone.

Frank and Norman emptied the cotton into the bed of the big truck, throwing the empty sacks back to the ground. The help gathered them up and with water jar in hand, headed for the pickup. Everyone, except the crew boss. He lingered behind to talk with Robert to collect his pay.

Robert knew if he had tried to pay the pickers less, there would be trouble. He figured he could handle one crew boss.

"I pay extra for clean cotton. I'm going to pay you half, that's all."

The man looked at Robert for a moment

before taking the pay. He shook his head as he returned to his truck. Alex heard him say, "It ain't right, it just ain't right."

He left, snatching the changing of gears as he made it out of the field. He was gone, Alex could breathe now. It was time to take the local help home.

"Did you see how he looked at me?"

"Yes, sir," Alex was fast to say, "I didn't like him."

"Me neither, not one bit," Robert said.

Pulling to a stop, June Bug was the first one off the truck. The rest of his family followed, in a slow, stove up sort of way.

Robert waved. "See y'all in the morning."

Ester waved, the only one to do so. She stood for a moment before climbing onto the porch. With the look of pain, she stretched her back and pressed it against the palm of her hand. A narrow sided hound dog lay under the porch. In the yard, a red rooster pecked at the dirt.

On the way home, Alex thought about June Bug, and his lunch, the little he had.

"What do they eat for supper, daddy?"

"I never thought about it."

"When June Bug gets old enough, what school will he go to?"

"Not ours," Robert said.

"I'm glad we don't live in a shack. I feel sorry for June Bug."

"You got a lot to learn about blacks. They want to live like that. They are used to it."

"Do they... have a school bus?"

"You ask too many questions. I want you to stop playing with him, it doesn't look right."

Alex said nothing else, he knew what his daddy meant. He liked playing with June Bug, but he could never be like him, even if, he wanted to.

It was getting dark by the time they returned home. Out at the barn, the lights of the two-ton went dim, Frank had finished parking it for the night. He was fourteen and had been driving since Alex could remember.

Robert did not allow Norman to get behind the wheel. It was not his age, being a few years younger than Frank. He was just too short. Norman was not like the rest, not in looks, nor in speech. He was not stupid, maybe slow, but not stupid.

Amy waited on the porch.

"I missed you," she said, kissing Robert.

Amy was almost six. Alex thought she was cute when she was born, not anymore. Alex was always with his daddy until Amy was there.

Who needs them? Alex thought, as he reached to pet his dog, Buster. His mother would be in the kitchen. Alex hurried.

It was a peaceful place to be, sitting in the corner of the kitchen, his back against the wall. There were one hundred and eight squares of black and white tile, counting the ones under the cabinets, soon he would count them again.

He enjoyed watching his mother. Her eyes were brown, and her hair jet black, cut just past the shoulders. Her name was Sandra, she was just about the best mama a boy could have.

"Been a short summer," his mother said, "I will miss having you around."

Alex did not say much about his school, about third grade.

"I rather stay with you?"

"Don't you want to see your friends?"

"I don't need friends. I have Buster and June Bug."

"You know how your daddy feels about that. Want to help me set the table? You can get the glasses."

Mr. Baker gave them away. Of course, you had to fill up with gas to get one. Gas was three gallons for a dollar.

Sandra said grace, with prayers too long. Alex hoped that the Lord paid more attention to her prayers than they did. If it were up to Alex, he would have said, "Thank you, Lord," and called it a day. However, everyone kept quiet about it. Sandra was the only one that wanted the job.

After the amen, Frank was quick to get in the first word, "Mama we got almost a half truckload today. And…"

Alex interrupted, "Daddy fired the crew boss, he was mean."

"Your daddy or the crew boss?"

Robert looked up in time to see Sandra shift her eyes toward him. His face stern now, glancing down at Alex, "Eat your supper, your mama don't care what goes on in the field."

"Robert, you should know better, not with all that is going on. They are already marching in Alabama. That King fellow has got them all stirred up."

"Pass the biscuits. I don't care if I make them mad. I won't have an uppity crew boss cheat me."

"Why does Amy get to stay here?" Brushing Alex aside for the moment, he continued, "You got to draw the line somewhere."

With the look of aggravation, he returned to Alex, "Stop asking that, I told you, she is too young. Her birthday is in December, she will have to stay here with your mama."

And with you, Alex thought, getting up from the table.

The Morgans lived in the Bible Belt. Sundays were set aside for church. There were plenty to choose from Baptist, Methodist, and the Church of God. Sermons ranged from short and quiet, too long and loud if you were in the Church of God.

Alex's granddaddy went to the Baptist church, a distinguished group, with no carrying on, saying amen and such.

Robert went to the same church and was baptized down by the creek, said the preacher near bout froze him to death. He switched over to the Church of God when he started going with Sandra. He never did get baptized in the same way Alex's mother did. Sandra was baptized in the Holy Ghost, whatever that means.

At her church, the men or at least a few of them wore white shirts with stomachs poked out between suspenders. Men of spiritual authority, sanctified men, the kind that could spot a sinner a mile away.

Most of the women were plain Jane. They wore no makeup, jewelry, or anything else that could make them look better. All seemed short of money for a haircut, the way they bunched their hair up in a bun.

Sandra, like all good middle-class folks, kept a Family Bible on the coffee table. It was large and white, gold letters on top. She bought it from a young Bible salesman. They came around on Saturdays, with a sob story in one hand and a Bible in the other.

Church service remained the same. During the summer months, unless it was raining, the windows were always left open. Funeral fans were the only relief from the heat and gnats. Right above the fan handle was the ad for dead people.

If the funeral fan did not remind you of the dead, the preacher would. He talked about people dying all the time, shouting things like, "If you think it is hot in here, wait till you get to hell."He seemed to enjoy, running up and down the aisle, throwing people into hell just so he could pull them out again with talk too long.

The services ended the same, the same people stuttering and a falling down, playing dead. Elders covered the women with blankets. Later, the preacher prayed for them to get up and go home. With all the chattering, and thrashing about, they appeared haggard, and no better off than before.

TED VICK

CHAPTER 2

Alex believed God was white, unlike June Bug and his kind. Their churches were easy to spot, long names and sagging picnic tables under pine trees.

Alex had asked him if he wanted to go fishing? If he knew a place? It surprised him that June Bug worried about his mother and what she would say. He might as well have said, no.

"There's a fishing spot on Levi's place. We don't go. Mama said he's crazy. He carries a gun in his back pocket. If you go down there, you better be careful."

There were rumors about Levi and his wife. Some said she left him, others said, she disappeared. Whether, she went during the night, without so much as a goodbye, or just vanished, Alex did not know. Strange things happen behind closed doors.

Levi had an eighteen acre farm, the least of any in the community. He worked the land with a mule and plow. Few people, white or black, had anything to do with him.

Alex did not remember ever seeing anyone with him. The few times they saw him in public, Alex did not speak to him, nor did his daddy. Alex guessed Levi was too good for his people and not good enough for anyone else.

He decided to ask Levi about fishing, but not in front of his daddy. Alex figured Levi wasn't crazy enough to pull a gun on a white boy.

With a fishing pole in hand, Alex told his mother, he would be back in time for supper. With a smile, she wished him luck. Too busy to ask Alex any questions, she turned back to her work,

Excited to see something new, he walked without slowing. Less than an hour later, he turned off the main road, onto the lane to Levi's house. It was more like a path through a field than a means of travel. His mother said it was good to walk the narrow road. She had not seen this one, he thought, as sandspurs reached for the fray of his blue jeans.

The house had the look of emptiness, built with planks of gray and twisted lumber.

The chimney, cracked in places, held onto the house, despite the constant pull of gravity. Soot, black in color, covered the top flue and streaks of it ran down like mascara on a tear-stained face.

The front door was without paint, matching the rest of the house. A pair of rusty hinges held the frame windows in place. They opened like shutters, the two that Alex could see. Beams that once held the porch level, now weak with age, and rotted in height, sloped toward the ground.

The dog on the porch was quick to stand, barking now, with hair raised. Levi was out back, he walked around to see what all the fuss was about.

"Settle down Boo, it's nothing but a boy," he said.

There was no gun that he could see.

"Who you be?"

"Alex from down the road, I stopped by to see if, well, reckon I could go fishing?"

"Ah, Mr. Morgan's boy."

"Yes, sir."

"You look too young to be fishing by yourself?"

"I am nine. Daddy don't care."

"Fishing… all you want from me?"

"I don't let people do any fishing on my place. But, I guess, you won't cause any trouble."

"No, sir."

His dog laid back down, with perked ears, and wide eyes.

"It's over yonder on the backside of the field," Levi said, pointing.

"By the way, I can't remember the last time anyone called me sir," Levi said, as Alex walked away.

In time, Alex realized that Levi wasn't crazy, he was just like him. He went back often. Soon, Levi's dog Boo greeted him with the movements of a runaway clock.

The yard, just plain dirt. Levi swept it with a broom, made out of dog fennel and twigs wrapped with haywire. Levi said it was not just for looks. Tracks, be it a man or a snake, made during the night, were easier to see. Levi hated snakes. The last thing he wanted was a rattler living under his house.

He did not have much, in the way of possessions, not on the outside and from what Alex could see from the porch, not on the inside. A table with a kerosene lantern, and three chairs, and a fireplace with a candle on the mantle, that was about it. He did have a Bible, not fancy and white, just plain and black.

Alex liked his mule, Molly. She was big for a two-year-old. Levi built her a shed next to the corn crib. He made it with second-hand tin, and pine slab spaced too far apart. It looked too small for Molly, the roof stood no more than a foot above her head. During summer showers, the hot tin turned raindrops into steam.

"Don't she get tired?" Alex asked as he touched Molly's brown hair.

"We both do. I take it easy, plow her shallow. She won't be able to pull deep until she gets about five years old. We take a two-hour break at lunch and plenty of water breaks. Anyone tells you they can plow a mule all day, ain't plowed with one."

"Why don't you get a tractor?"

"No money. Besides, we're family. I can't picture myself talking to a tractor."

"You're right, I rather talk to Molly, she looks better."

He only saw Levi in one pair of overalls, the same ones all the time, torn at the knees. The hole in his right pocket mended with white thread. He joked that he put his name on it so everyone would know they belonged to him.

There were no cuffs above his army boots, boots with souls worn one-sided, and strings knotted to short.

Each morning he outfitted Molly with bridle and bit and the weight of the collar, harness, frame, and backing band, and a plow that haunted her every step.

There was little need to yell git... up and gee... haw, Molly knew where she was going, which way to turn. Alex saw them, more than once plowing in the distance, working until the sun faded behind the tall Georgia pines.

There wasn't much Alex could say about Frank. He was tall and skinny, the only one with blonde hair. Frank was mean to people and animals too. He killed a cat once. Alex saw him do it, shot him out of a tree, for no reason. He was a yellow tabby. Alex had no trust in a person that hated cats.

Frank asked Alex to go fishing with him. It seemed odd, it was much too late in the day for a fishing trip.

It didn't take long before Frank turned the truck onto a dirt lane just past the "African-American To God be the Glory Baptist Church."

"Is this where you have been going?"

Frank laughed as he skidded the rear tires of the truck into the sandy ditch and out again. Going too fast toward the end of the road, he slammed on the brakes, stopping only inches from a magnolia tree.

They opened their doors, to the swallow of dirt, and the smell of dust.

"Boo, stop barking, it's okay," Alex heard Levi say.

Levi quit rocking and stared for a moment, then turned his eyes back again to the white porcelain pan in his lap. Unsettled, he shifted his weight. Without saying a word, he returned to the snapping of string beans.

"I have to talk to Levi, to ask him if it is all right."

"Nah, come on, it is getting late."

Frank gathered the fishing poles and bait. Levi had gone inside.

"Please, Frank, we got to ask him."

"Why? It's just old Levi."

"He is not that old, and this is his farm."

"Shut up, Alex. I don't want to hear it."

They fished for less than an hour. Alex was not in the mood for fishing, and Frank, all he wanted was to drive the truck. It was dark when they returned to Levi's place.

He was standing in the doorway. The kerosene lamp on the table was the only light in the house. Levi looked ten feet tall as the shadows fell past him and into the yard.

Alex interrupted Frank's stare, "Do you see the dog?"

"No. Why?"

"She is mean, bite me once, got the blood."

Frank looked around at his feet, threw his pole in the truck, and hurried to the cab.

On the way home, Alex told Frank all about Levi.

"You know, June Bug said he's crazy."

"Do you really, think he is?"

"Maybe. He totes a gun, a thirty-eight."

"I have never seen a black person with a pistol. I think it's against the law?"

"All I know is, Levi has one."

Frank was quick to reply, "He knows better than mess with me."

"He killed people in the war."

"Why didn't you tell me?"

"Well…. It never came up before."

"You didn't get close enough to see him do it, but he looks strange when he twitches."

"Twitches?"

"Yeah, his mouth curls up a bit in the corner. His bottom lip kinda flutters like."

Frank asked no more questions. Alex was smart with mind games, he had watched his mother and father. They did it all the time.

Alex walked down the lane to Levi's place. Frank showing his butt the day before was still on his mind. What was he going to say? How could he tell Levi, Frank don't like black people? I can't tell him that. I have to put it another way. Maybe I should go back and not say anything?

A summer shower, it came out of nowhere. Instead of turning back, Alex ran to Levi's porch.

"Mr. Morgan, I didn't expect to see you back so soon. Where is your pole?"

"Frank, I need to tell you about Frank. He is mean, he mistreats people. He had no business coming here. I did not want him to. I don't want you to be mad at me."

"Slow down…. Catch your breath, too late in the day to be in such a hurry. There ain't nobody mad at you. I know what you are talking about. But, there is no need to feel sad about it, people do things to one another, that is life. I don't waste my time worrying about it too much."

"I worry about everything, no matter how much I try, nothing turns out right."

"Alex, you are too hard on yourself, life gets broken, not you or anyone else can fix it. There are some things you have to live with."

"Was it any better when you were a boy?"

"If you mean what I think you do, it was better in a way. Folks were more accepting of their place, we had trouble, but not like it is nowadays. I never believed in tearing something up, just because it belongs to someone else. If you got your hand out, mama always said you better have a hoe in it. There is no shame in hard work."

"Did you grow up on a farm?"

"Yes, sir. We were sharecroppers, lived out in the middle of nowhere. We didn't own much, a mule and wagon, a few pots and pans, that was about it."

Alex spoke, without thought, "Daddy said, only poor people sharecrop."

Levi smiled. He knew Alex didn't mean anything by it. "I reckon you are right. All of us are poor in one way or another, some just don't know it yet."

"If I were rich enough to travel, I would like to see the ocean," Alex said.

"When I was your age, I saw it. Daddy took us to Savannah a few times, it took near a day, we always camped out on the way back. We stayed off the main road, daddy made sure of that. He had a saying, 'out of sight, out of trouble.'

"Speaking of trouble, as far as what Frank did, I want you to forget about it."

"I wish I could be like that, I don't forget about stuff. Look what Frank did."

Alex opened his shirt and showed Levi his scar, about the size of a dime it was.

"Your brother? He did that?"

"Yes, sir. He said I was bothering them. I only wanted to hear what him and Norman were saying. Frank motioned me to the truck. Without saying a word, he used me for an ashtray. It happened so fast there was no time to jump back. I remember hearing my skin sizzle. What they did to me wasn't right.

"Daddy said he was sorry, but I shouldn't been aggravating Frank. Said I didn't know when to stop."

Levi looked as if he wanted to say something about it. Instead, he shook his head.

"He did worse things to Norman. He tried to set him on fire."

Levi leaned forward in his rocker, "He did what?"

"Yes, sir. It happened last fall. They snuck off to the barn without me. By the time I got there, Norman was under the shed, working on his bicycle, and Frank was building a fire beneath the chinaberry tree.

"I told him. I could get some more wood. But, he yelled for me to get back to the house. I stood there. I was tired of being ordered around. Frank got mad and went into the shed.

"In a few minutes, I heard them fussing. Norman ran into the yard. Frank, with a rope in his hand, ran after him. Roped him like a cow, and dragged him, feet first over to the tree. He threw the rope over a limb and pulled until Norman's head was a few feet above the ground.

"Frank told me he was going to put Norman in the fire. Said, it would be my fault for not going back to the house.

"With a pull and a push, he swung Norman through the flames."

"Stop it. I thought you were joking?" Norman yelled.

"Frank managed a nervous laugh as he untied Norman."

"Stop crying," Frank said, "I didn't hurt you none, just scorched your hair a bit."

"Mama and Daddy didn't think it was so funny. Frank got a beating that night."

"I bet your brother was mad?"

"Norman? He did not say one bad word about Frank. I couldn't figure it out, found out the truth the next day. I told Frank, he was cruel to swing Norman over the fire."

"You got to be stupid? How do you think I could do all that to Norman? He was in on it, we wanted to scare you. It was all a setup, and you fell for it."

"That was a bad thing he did to your brother. Don't like to see nobody burnt, saw too much of that in war."

"You ever kill anybody? I told Frank you did, I tried to put a scare in him."

"I did what I had to do. There's not any fun in the killing."

"By the way, has the store truck stopped by your place?" Levi said.

"Do they have candy?"

"He sales a lot of stuff. The 'skinny-man' is what we call him. If he stops, keep your distance, he is strange."

Alex gave heed to the concern in Levi's voice. He didn't tell his daddy, Alex knew he wouldn't want to hear anything about what Levi had to say. His daddy had said, "Levi was a farmer, not like them, just a farmer."

TED VICK

Chapter 3

*E*veryone had his place, Levi on his farm, the people in the cotton patch, even the person coming down the road that day.

It was the man Levi had warned him about. He was slow to pull into the yard. The truck had cracked paint and rusted fenders. A steady stream of smoke rattled its way out of the tailpipe. It was tied up low to the ground with a piece of haywire.

"Good evening, sir, I'm Sam, the man from New Orleans."

He made the mistake of extending his hand.

"You can call me Sam."

The greeting was reluctant, at best.

"I'm staying at the old Simmons house. Figured I would get out and meet my new neighbors. I got fruit, candy, and soft drinks to sell. I call it my 'Rolling Store.'"

"Not today," Robert said, turning away.

"Yes, sir. Maybe later, sir."

He looked sad as he closed the tailgate. He left

with the promise to return in a few weeks.

All Robert could talk about at supper, was the stranger.

"Did you see how he pulled his truck into the yard? Like, he owned the place."

"I got news for him, I am not his neighbor. There ain't nobody living in the Simmons shack going to call me, neighbor. He might be from New Orleans, but he is still black."

Frank chimed in, "I thought people from New Orleans have an accent. That fellow is no more from New Orleans than I am."

"He might be a high yellow. A full-blooded black wouldn't dare be so quick as to shake my hand."

"Robert, you're going to get into trouble one day. They have feelings just like us."

"Not like me?"

"Maybe you are right Robert, you don't have any feelings."

"Are we going to start that again?" Robert said, getting up from the table. Leaving tea in his glass.

The anger inside his daddy was also in Alex. It did not show up as often, but it was there, hiding in the darkness of his mind, waiting for an ill deed or misspoken word.

He never had a reason to dislike Joe, his classmate. He didn't mean to push him so hard, that day at the edge of the playground. But, he did. And nothing could be done to take it back.

A few of the boys gathered to see what would happen next.

"Are you crazy? What made you push me like that?"

Alex turned mean. People had said that about his mother. With the back of his hand, he slapped Joe, on one side of his face and then the other. Some of the boys yelled for him to stop. Alex knew then, he had gone too far.

Alex turned and walked away. His emptiness was now filled with shame. Why did I do that?

The next day Alex stood near the teacher's desk, his hands pressed against a window of small panes with metal frames in a wall of block and mortar. And unlike the windows, this room had no hold on him.

Joe came in and sat down at his desk, his face swollen. Alex figured Joe's parents were in the principal's office. He waited for the teacher to call out his name. She never did.

After lunch, Alex saw Joe sitting on the bench by the side of the building. He was alone, staring at a cat-eye marble. Alex hesitated. He knew he should say something to Joe, but what?"

"Nice marble...Joe, I'm so sorry I hurt you. You were right, I just when a little crazy."

"Mama said I should tell the principal."

"Why didn't you?"

"It still hurts some but you getting a beating won't help me none. One day, I want to be a preacher like my daddy. I guess a person has to start somewhere."

Joe looked back at his marble.

The last bell of the day, Alex wasted no time getting out the door. Steps of silver and diamond plate were waiting in the parking lot. It was an old bus with the name of the school in faded paint.

The seats were Naugahyde. Ugly brown, with torn corners that revealed springs of iron, naked except for, a spot of rust here and there.

The noise of chatter without end drove Alex to sit alone, in the back of the bus. His house was five miles away. He looked past the dirt on the window into a world beyond his view, a world of dreams.

The bus swayed as it turned onto the dirt of the road, his house in view. It was his time to take part in the rhythm of stopping and pausing, and the door opening and closing. Norman and Frank got off with him. The bus smoked and jerked with the change of each gear as it headed for the next stop.

Alex was glad to put the school day behind him. He hurried across the yard and up the steps, where square columns stood, two on each side. The window of his bedroom looked out upon the porch of gray, planked wood. It was just a room, shared with brothers, a place to sleep and to change clothes, nothing more.

The screen door slammed behind him. Unlike last week, the living room was quiet, the birdcage in the corner was empty now. The sound of breathing and moving about was gone.

Mr. Atkins, the owner of the Five and Dime, had given Alex's mother, two parakeets. She said he had grown tired of them. The way Robert acted, there might have been something more.

"Alex, the birds are for you and Amy. I hope they will teach y'all how to get along with each other."

"Do they have to stay in the cage?"

"That is the only place they have ever known."

"Can we let them out to play?"

"No, if they escape, they will die, please be careful, Alex."

The birds played at first, excited to be in a new place, until Amy began to torment them, poking her finger between the bars, jabbing at them, they moved, she moved. The male became aggressive.

Alex was glad the bird pecked Amy. Daddy's little girl deserved it.

"They are mean, I don't want them anymore."

"Fine, keep your fat fingers out of their cage."

Alex thought they would play again. He was wrong. The birds seemed sad now, unable to forget Amy's abuse. There was nothing else he could do, beyond giving them food and water.

"Mama, they don't seem happy, they cry all the time."

"They are not crying, just fussing a little, that's all."

They screamed all day, Friday. Alex covered the cage, hoping they would sleep.

The next morning, Alex found one curled in the corner. The blood on her head had already dried.

His mother came in from feeding the chickens.

"Amy told me what happened. I'm sorry about your bird. What did you do with it?

"It was a girl. I buried her in the shade, in the corner of the yard."

"She must have been sick."

"No, mama. The boy bird killed her. It is Amy's fault, the way she treated them."

The other bird stopped eating. A few days later, Alex peered to see, to see if he was all right, this bird dressed in bright colors of green and blue. On newspaper print, he stood, and with the slant of his head, he moved his eye up and toward Alex.

There was no sound of singing, only the silence of his crying. Why would he kill his mate and then mourn her death? Alex looked for an answer, and in the bird's eye, he saw his own reflection. At that moment, he knew what the bird wanted. Alex gave him the same freedom he had given his mate.

Alex opened his hand. The bird hesitated, and then the air was beneath his wings. He flew as if he was born to fly, soaring high into the blue sky. Then he disappeared into the trees along the edge of the yard. Did I do the right thing? Lord, please take care of him.

His mother was at the door when he returned to the house.

"Alex, what have you done. I told you not to let him loose."

"I felt sorry for him. He told me he wanted to leave, to live with the other birds in the trees."

"Alex, what am I going to do with you? Sometimes you are too kind-hearted. Tell you what, we will remember him in our prayers. God said he takes care of the sparrows, I reckon that means parakeets too."

That night, just before sleep, Alex covered his head, with breath against the whiteness of the sheet. It was his private place, a world of dreams and things not ordinary. He thought about Joe and the bird. How do I have such power, to do at will, acts of hate and kindness?

CHAPTER 4

The brass cage in the corner looked out of place, sad in its emptiness, hanging with no purpose. Alex begged his mama not to get any more birds. It was a good time for Alex to get out of the house, away to his own space.

However, no matter how far Alex walked down the dirt road, his mind kept spinning with thoughts of Joe's face, swollen blue, and the bird of yellow and green.

He looked down. With each step, curls of dust rose between his toes, turning the white strings of his faded jeans to a dull red. One-step, two-step, three step, four, then again and again.

The ditch diggers were by his house early that morning. Alex spent the afternoon following in the tracks of the road grader, looking for coke bottles in the fresh mounds of dirt. Mr. Baker paid a penny a bottle. Not much, but enough to by two shortbread cookies.

Without notice, the light of day, faded. The

evening sky, painted in colors of red and yellow, cast an orange glow on the standing fields of corn. Streams of light filtered through the green needles of longleaf pine, until the last of its colors faded beyond the darkness of the night.

A car passed by, leaving Alex behind in the dust. In the distance, the once bright tail lights of the vehicle grew dim. The hedgerows on both sides closed in upon him, and like a witch's spell, the air turned into a creepy haze.

Someone was coming, Alex turned around to see a halo of headlights. Like a dusty ghost, a pickup came into view. The stopping, the sound of brakes worn thin. It was the 'skinny man'. The ditch. There was no other choice. It was the only place to hide. He was glad Buster was not there.

The truck slowed to a complete stop. Alex froze at the squeak of rusty hinges and a door not closing. Then the cry of rock pebbles beneath steps, uneven steps, making their way toward the back of the pickup.

A smoker's voice broke the silence of the evening air. The man was a few feet past him now, his thin frame lit by the dim glow of tail lights covered in layers of dusty clay.

"Is that you, Alex? You know I have the power, the power to see you in the dark."

Levi was right, he was strange, why else would

he say he could see in the dark. Alex stayed still. There was silence as his breath retreated beneath the pounding of his heart. He saw the shaking of the exhaust pipe, close enough to feel ribbons of warm air upon his face.

"Do you want a ride?"

Alex stayed silent.

He repeated it. Losing patience, he returned to his ragged truck seat and slammed the door shut. First gear growled back until it found its match and then he was gone, leaving behind the smell of burnt oil.

Alex pulled himself out of the ditch and onto the road. He was slow to stand, the images of the skinny man remained in his mind. I got to get home.

Biting his bottom lip, he took a deep breath, aware of his bare chest. His mind told him in repeated voice, I am brave and not afraid. And then, he ran, running past the blackberry bushes, down toward the creek, the wind in his face.

He did not stop until he reached the bridge, an old bridge with a skeleton of twisted and broken lumber sagging toward the creek bed below.

Alex had never been this late before. He looked around, not that he was afraid of the gator that lived under the bridge, the one Frank had seen. He just didn't see any need of stepping on him. The ruma-bum of a bullfrog and bushes that moved caused him to hurry across. Not seeing his step, his foot gave way to a plank of rotten wood, he fell forward, and then, the hurt of stopping.

Blood ran down his face, and onto his lips, the taste and smell turned his stomach. His mouth was dry, and dryer still as he listened to the water in the creek as it flowed beneath the bridge, beneath him.

His breath slowed, and his thoughts, like balloons escaped to an empty sky. Then, the touch of a hand, the breath of drink, and the smell of sweaty arms. There was a groan and some hesitation. Alex's body gave way to the hurry of step, and the slam of a door, then another and a motor slow to start.

Blurred memories, of time and space, followed Alex into a familiar place. His head felt heavy as it descended into a pillow of softness and the smell of fresh cotton.

Alex heard his name rise from a sea of muffled sound and awoke to see his daddy leaning over, pinning his shoulders to the bed.

"I hurt. Where's mama?"

"Hold still."

Hands, that of a stranger grabbed his leg, jerking it forward. Alex screamed at the snap of his knee. It was over, his leg was free to fall back to the sheet of the bed.

"The shot will knock him out."

Frank was the next voice he heard, telling him to wake up, and that Daddy was mad.

"What happened on the bridge? You better come up with a good story."

He was thirsty, the pain was still in his knee. His mother walked into the room.

"I told you to let him sleep."

"He woke up. It wasn't my fault."

"How are you doing darling? Here, drink some water."

"My knee hurts."

"The doctor said it would just take time to heal. He set your leg last night."

"Alex, what happened?"

"Running on the bridge. I slipped. Did daddy come and get me?"

"Levi brought you home."

"My head, is it cut bad? Will I have headaches? I don't want to take shots."

"No baby, not like your daddy."

"Stop running in and out of the room," Sandra said, turning her attention to Norman and Amy.

"Everyone, out. That includes you, Frank. Alex needs to rest."

Later, Alex was awakened by the sound of a horn. Alex looked out the bedroom window. It was Levi parked by the edge of the road, his door part way opened.

Sandra was with Alex when Robert returned.

"What did Levi want?"

"He wanted to see Alex, I told him he was asleep."

Alex knew his daddy had lied to Levi. He was not welcome to come into the house unless his daddy needed labor fitting to a black. If it was to help Alex feel better, that was different.

"Did you thank him for bringing our boy home?"

"I thanked him, and that's all. He probably thought I owed him something. I don't want to talk any more about it."

Robert closed the door behind him. Alex was glad to be alone with his mother. She held my hand and prayed for Levi and me.

A few weeks later, Levi came by again, this time Alex was in the front yard.

"How is that leg, Mr. Morgan?"

"It don't hurt no more."

"I near bout ran over you. There you were, laying in the road like a dead possum."

"Mama said God uses people to help us when there's no angel close by."

"I been called a lot of things, but never an angel. You know I ain't no angel."

The Church of God had no use for fun. They didn't have any and were jealous if anyone who did. When it came to picture shows the Baptists were just as bad.

It was different for Alex's mother, she was all for having a good time. It was strange, seeing how she was a church member and all.

The aroma of popcorn lured Alex into the kitchen.

"Why are you putting it away?"

"I'm saving it for tonight," she smiled.

"Go change into some clean clothes. We are going to the movies."

'Young people kissing and a sinning. The drive-ins are the gates of hell.' That is what the preacher had said. This time Alex was going to have a closer look.

All the family went, except Frank. Alex figured it had something to do with the pickup.

At the edge of town, Robert pulled the car over to the side of the road. He looked around, for a moment, before getting out and opening the door to the backseat.

"Alex, hurry, you and Norman know what to do."

Robert unlocked the trunk. It was just big enough. They bunched up together, Alex's head was next to the tire jack, he moved to stop the hurting.

Robert saw lights, without another word, he slammed the lid shut. In a moment, they were back on the highway.

"Norman, are you scared? It is pitch dark in here. Answer me, are you over there?"

"Where else do you think I am? Stupid."

"I told you I didn't want to do this. Will we really go to jail if we get caught?"

"Shut up. When we get to the movie gate, you better not cough."

In a short time, Alex felt the turning of the car. Gravel crunched beneath the wheels as they rolled to a stop. He covered his mouth, trying not to breathe, much less cough.

Alex heard someone walk around to the back of the car. They were caught, the lid would open at any moment.

Then a voice, an uneasy voice.

"Nice night for a movie. Just, the three of you?"

"No, just the wife and me. Our little girl is only four."

"I'm sorry, I thought she was older. There will be no charge for her. Can't be too careful nowadays, people sneak in, you know?"

"Yes, sir. Some people you can't trust."

"That will be a dollar and a half."

Robert drove to the back of the parking lot.
Alex was ready to get out of the trunk. He heard
other cars parking, doors slamming, and people
talking. Then, there was less noise.

"I hope daddy lets us out soon? What if we run
out of air?"

"You ask the most questions. The short answer,
dead people, don't watch movies."

The lock turned, popping the lid part way.
"Come on, hurry," Robert said. Not slowing he
returned to the front seat. Alex crawled out of the
trunk. I thought it would be darker. The girl in
the car next to them, smiled as she looked over
the shoulder of the guy she was with. Hot dog, the
preacher was right.

"Stop staring, get in the car," Norman said.

Alex turned his attention to the screen. Bambi
was on that night. The kids at school had talked
about it. Alex hoped they were wrong about it being
sad.

Minutes later, the manager made it clear, Robert had cheated him.

"Just making sure, everything is all right," said
the man, appearing at Robert's window.

"Yes, sir."

He bent down, shining his light into the back.

Alex moved into the corner of the seat, putting
his face into the fabric cover. We are going to jail.

"You are lucky to have such a fine looking bunch of kids. My wife and I can't have children. I hope they enjoy the movie."

Alex looked up in time to see the man staring at his daddy. With the look of wanting to say more, he walked away.

Amy whispered to Sandra. "I think I wet my pants."

The movie started just as Sandra and Amy were returning from the bathroom.

"I'm glad we have our own popcorn, the price at the concession stand is outrageous."

"Highway robbery is what it is," Robert said, as he lit the tiny green tree hanging on the rearview mirror. "I sure hope the smoke keeps the mosquitoes away."

Alex tried not to think about it, the sadness of the movie. He watched the girl next door. She seemed pretty happy.

"Don't say anything about us sneaking into the show, some people might not understand," Robert said on the way home.

Later, Sandra reminded Alex not to forget his prayers. The prayer she taught him didn't help. *Now I lay me down to sleep. If I die before I wake, I pray the Lord, my soul to take.*

There were things Alex feared, death was one of those things.

In a dream, Alex saw a man in the woods with a gun, standing by an open grave. Was it because of the movie? Or, what he had seen near the cypress swamp? In the middle of a thicket. A hole dug the size of a human grave, about three feet deep.

Then came December. Amy was busy complaining about the pine tree in the living room. Alex had placed it in the corner, next to the fireplace.

"Mama, that tree is downright ugly."

"It won't be when it is decorated. After supper, you can help me string up some popcorn."

"Daddy said it's lopsided."

"You and your daddy, y'all never see good in anything. I don't want to hear another word about the tree."

Alex walked back into the kitchen with his mother.

"Where did you find such a pretty tree?"

"By the pond. You really like it?"

"Of course I do, it sure does smell good."

"Black people, do they have Christmas like we do?"

"Can't really say. I think so."

"I need to ask June Bug if he believes in Santa like Amy. What if he asks for something and he don't get it? Cause, his family is so poor."

"He doesn't get it."

"Yes. ma'am."

"Why are you so worried about what black people do?"

"Oh, nothing…. Some things just get stuck in my mind."

However, Alex had a reason to ask. He wanted to do the right thing by Levi.

Closing the top flap of his jacket tight around his neck, he hurried down the lane. In the distance, black smoke rose from the chimney. Must have fat lightered a going. Alex hoped Levi would invite him inside.

Behind the door, Boo started barking. When Levi heard it was Alex, he was quick to open the door.

"Why you be out in this kind of weather?"

"To see how y'all are doing. I got presents."

"Boy, come on in here before you catch a sickness."

Levi pulled up another chair to the warmth of the fire. Boo sat down beside Alex's chair, sniffing the croaker sack in his lap.

"I brought Boo a ham bone, do you want me to give it to her outside?"

"No, sir. Just throw it on the floor, the grease might shine it up a bit."

"I'll be right back, I got Molly something."

Alex took an apple out of the bag and ran to the crib. In no time at all, he was back.

"That didn't take long?"

"No. Sir. Not cause of the cold, Molly is just a fast eater."

"One gift left. It is for you," Alex said, reaching into the sack, handing Levi his present.

"Boy, this thing is heavy as a rock."

"It is a rock, I found it in a field."

Levi unwrapped it with a grin. "Never seen a rock with seashells and little critter drawings all over it."

"A fossil, that's what it is, we are studying fossils in school. My teacher has a little one, she was proud of it until I showed her mine."

"Don't know anyone, I rather give it to."

"Tell you what Alex, when I die, you can have it back."

"Die?"

"Come on now, don't look so sad. Old Levi is not going anywhere, not yet. I figure you and me, we got a lot more talking to do."

"I hate the thought of dying. Why would God want to kill us?"

"I don't know the answer. Maybe God wants to

surprise us with a gift of His own. Dying could be His way of saying you got to close your eyes first."

"I don't like the dark."

"Alex, there are a lot of happy things we can talk about. We sure do thank you for the presents."

"Since you like old things…."

Levi got his Bible from the mantel, a large Bible, with worn edges and faded letters on the top.

"We can sit over here," Levi said.

Alex joined him at the table. Near the back cover was an envelope, yellowed with age. Levi took the contents, four pages in total and pressed them against the wood top.

"My great-grandma wrote this letter a long time ago," Levi said, pointing to the date in the upper, right-hand corner: 1890

"It is old, I wasn't even here then," Alex said.

Levi read it aloud.

To my children that be in the world now. There is no truth in what some say. We were not all treated bad. I have no reason to complain. They say we were snatched in the night from our family. It ain't so. To those who whine, wishing to go back across the water. Nothing there, people eating monkey meat and running bout naked. Headhunters took my brother. I run off to the forest. My mother. They killed.

"Headhunters, I know about headhunters. Got a book from school."

Levi stopped to put another log on the fire, as Alex waved his hands about, his eyes wide with excitement.

"Calm down, boy. No need to get all excited and such."

"I just like natives and jungles."

"You would not like it if you knew what goes on, deep in the woods when darkness falls. My great-grandmother said she was twelve when the slave traders captured her, the same color, but from a different tribe. They took her to the coast, kept her tied to a post for a week until the tall boat came."

He continued.

They pushed us into the ship across a board, like a chicken to her pen. We clung to one another. No room to do any different. The men walked above us on planks of wood carrying light in their hands. The ship's floor was damp and cold. The woman next to me died. It was a few days before they came and got her. The day before we landed they threw seawater into the cages. I remember the smell, I still do. Piles of our waste, too much to wash away. They gave us something to cover with. Mine was already torn. It was warmer than being naked.

We got here in 1858. Landed in a place I would later know, Jekyll Island. I could see land in the early morning light. They put us in small boats. It was the first time I ever saw a wagon or a mule. We went in different ways. I was glad not to be took very far. I heard later some were sold to a black man, he beat his slaves more than most.

God put me in the best place of all. Only ten of us on Mr. Gaines farm. His wife taught me to read and write. I stayed in the house, in a small room off the back porch. Kept their daughter. Pert near raised her as my own.

Mrs. Gaines told me about God. Read the Bible to me. I stayed with them. Sherman cared nothing about black people. Did what he was told. We hide out the pigs and chickens. They stole most everything else.

Mr. Gaines died and later his wife. They left the daughter everything except for five acres a piece to all the former slaves who were still living. There were three shacks on the place. I got one of my own. Raised two sons there.

Sometimes, God uses evil for good. And I am thankful God saved me a place on 'The Wanderer.' The last slave ship.

"That was a good story. My mama writes stories."

"I know…. You told me. Look at the time. You best be going, it will be dark soon."

"See you, Boo. You stay by the fire and take care of your daddy."

CHAPTER 5

*T*he warm spirit of Christmas faded into the cold of January. Down at the creek, fish swam beneath thin sheets of ice, as birds snuggled beneath the golden grass of barren fields.

"I want to bring Buster inside. He is going to freeze under the house."

"He will be warmer in his straw bed," his daddy said.

It was cold when the fire went out. Alex could not understand why his dog would be better off than they were? The three little pigs had it right. Why don't we all live in straw houses?

Buster was part bulldog, brown in color, with short stubby legs and a slobbering face. Sometimes, in the quiet of the night, he could hear him snoring. Alex could sleep, Buster was safe beneath the bedroom floor.

His mother had more time to spend at the kitchen table, a wooden table, covered with oilcloth, checkered in colors of red and white. She sat there, almost every night, writing her thoughts on a yellow note pad.

Robert said nothing about what Alex's mother was doing. Sandra told Alex if she ever sold any of the stories, she would let him read them, but only after, he got a little older.

Sandra seemed content. However, Robert became unsettled, sad. He mentioned selling the farm. It worried the rest of the family. Farming was the only life they had ever known.

Buster would not like it anyplace else. Alex had traveled to other places, in his mind, but to move Buster for no reason, it didn't make any sense.

Perhaps to Robert, Sandra was a little too happy. The preacher's wife, along with almost every other woman in the community, was jealous of Sandra. It didn't bother Alex. He liked having a good looking mama.

Concerned about the gossip, Robert questioned Sandra about everything. Then, it started again, the loud voices of his mother and father. It was their first fight since Christmas.

"I don't know what is wrong, that's the problem? All these years, I have tried to make you happy, I am so tired of trying," His daddy said.

"I'm happy, most of the time."

"You are with other people, and when you are writing, making up stories of a world, a world of going places and doing things I can't give you. This farm is all I have, and I know that is not enough. Maybe if we started over, someplace, this patch of dirt is all I have known, don't know if I could do anything else. It might be worth a try."

"I don't want to leave. I have friends here," Sandra said.

"You mean the preacher and the guy at the Five and Dime. I don't know of one woman friend you have. Oh, I forgot, Mrs. Baker, you have her."

"That's an ugly thing to say. You can be mean sometimes."

"Sandra, I have no more love to give you. I told you I loved you, said it every day, for years. There is nothing I can do that will satisfy you, not anymore."

"Just as I figured it is all my fault. It's late. I'm going back to bed."

Sometime past midnight, there was a stillness to the fussing. Robert stayed in the living room. Although he was alone, Alex heard him cursing his mother. Alex fell asleep. He did not know how long it was before his daddy went to bed, or if he ever did.

Morning came, and so did the clamber about the kitchen table. With no invitation to do so, his mother said nothing to Robert. In a rehearsed sort of way, lunches were packed, and good-byes said.

In a dusty cloud, the bus came dressed in its

yellow suit, stopping with the sound of squealing brakes. With quick steps, Alex left the porch and yard behind him, the bus driver greeted them, as if he too, wished to be somewhere else.

He hated going to school. Talking to his teacher and classmates was not something that would happen, not today. Seven hours later, Alex boarded the school bus for the trip back home.

Frank and Norman claimed their favorite seat. They said nothing when Alex passed by. He did not sit with them. Like his mama, he had no invitation to do so. The bus rounded the last curve, his mama waiting on the porch, she was all right.

Alex wondered why his daddy was out at the barn. Smoke was rising from the steel drum near the open shed. He went to see if anything was wrong.

Alex found him there, keeping warm by the open fire, without any reason or purpose in doing so.

"It is way too cold to be outside," Alex said.

"It is warmer out here."

"Warmer?"

"I mean, I rather be outside in the cold, than inside with a cantankerous woman. I should have listened to my daddy. He told me her family was nothing but white trash. Said, the only reason she wanted to marry me was to get a proper name."

"Mama is not white trash."

"That is what I thought, at first."

"She is right. You do say mean things."

"I was wrong to say that. I didn't get much sleep last night. As soon as y'all left for school, she started in at me, again."

I best not say anything to mama. The fighting has to end.

Robert's brother lived in Tampa. The mention of living there came up often. If that happened, Frank and Norman planned on cutting yards for a living. His daddy's dream was to own a fruit stand.

Uncle Bill and Aunt Peggy were both tall and skinny. She was a vegetarian, wormy in looks, never without words. Mama said she had no use for a woman that never shut up. Of course, Alex had heard his daddy say the same thing.

By letter, Sandra informed them that the family would go down for a visit. Arriving the next week on a Friday and staying until Monday.

Alex was glad to miss a few days of school, eating oranges right off the trees, what could be more exciting?

They crossed the Florida line. Billboards, all in a row as far as Alex could see. Some with pictures of half-naked girls on skis, and boats made of glass. His favorite sign: Alligators for sale. Alex wanted one of those baby alligators.

Robert pointed to a fruit stand by the side of the road. His voice echoed his excitement as he spoke of things he would do if he had his own fruit business.

"Frank, when you get old enough to drive on the highway, you can haul fruit while I stay and manage the business. Your mama is going to take care of the money."

"What about us, daddy?" Alex said.

"Why, that's the best part. You and Norman can help after school."

"I thought Frank and Norman were going to mow yards?"

"It depends on how close we live from town."

Amy looked nervous, "I think I wet my pants." Alex had heard that before.

They stopped at a store that sold pecans and souvenirs to the tourists. They advertised clean restrooms, the indoor kind.

While his mama was busy getting Amy a change of clothes. Alex, stared at the baby gators in the window.

Sandra had finished. She hurried back to the car with Amy. Not stopping, she looked over to Alex, "No, you can't have the alligator."

"I can put him in the washtub."

"I said no, let's get into the car."

His daddy chimed in. "Come on, Alex be careful, you might step on that bottom lip."

Once they were on the road again, his mother tried to explain.

"Alex, I wish you could have a baby alligator, but they won't stay little forever. Besides, we don't have the extra money. Gas is forty-five cents a gallon down here."

As they approached Tampa, cars were everywhere, in front, on the side and behind them, no one waved back. There were few pickup trucks in this sea of mean-looking people. Alex wanted to go back home. I don't like it here. I miss Buster.

Robert turned down one way and then another, and up the same road and back again. At last, he found the right street, all without having to ask for directions. He gave Sandra that I told you so look.

All the houses resembled one another with faded paint and neglect. Old people, old cars, even their dogs were old, not a young one in the bunch, did Alex see on this street, where his Uncle Bill lived. He could not imagine any of them paying someone to cut their grass.

Robert slowed to see the house numbers.

"We are here," Sandra said, "I don't see them. I hope they are home?"

Robert knocked on the door. Daddy was the only one smiling when Uncle Bill opened the door. After the hellos, and where is the bathroom? They gathered in the living room.

Alex listened, and so did everyone else. Everyone, except Aunt Peggy. The only time Robert and Uncle Bill had any peace was when she went into the kitchen.

In a few minutes, Aunt Peggy said supper was ready. She sure can cook fast, Alex thought.

"Sorry about the light meal. We didn't get to the store today."

That night was the first time Alex ever saw popcorn served as part of a meal. Everyone smiled and acted as if it was normal. Aunt Peggy stirred her salad before each bite while continuing to explain how good they were doing.

"I got a raise, Union work, that's where the money is," Uncle Bill said.

"Robert? How about your car, do you think it will make it back to Georgia? I'm about to trade mine for a new one."

"Our car, it will be just fine," Alex's mother said.

"I'm sure it will...Sandra."

His mother did not appreciate the sarcastic emphasis on her name, not by the look on her face.

After a few more awkward moments, the

grown-ups went into the living room, sending everyone else to bed. Alex's stomach was growling.

"Where are the oranges?" Alex said as he crawled under the cover.

"Shut up about the oranges," Frank said.

"Alex has a point. Where are the trees? And how are we going to make any money? The people look too old to care about a yard."

"I got to go again," Alex said.

He walked down the hall. It seemed strange to go in the house. Back home, he would be standing at the edge of the porch, talking to Buster.

On the way back, Alex overheard parts of a conversation.

"I was thinking about a fruit stand."

"Robert, how many fruit stands did you see coming down? They're everywhere. The last thing we need is another one."

"I told him that," Sandra said.

"Besides, the cost of living is high in Tampa," Uncle Bill said.

"We noticed the gas prices are out of sight," Sandra added.

"Both of you, stop it. I'm going to bed, we'll be heading back in the morning."

"Sorry, Robert. I would like nothing better than to have my brother close by."

Aunt Peggy was quick to say, "I enjoyed your

visit. I sleep late on Saturdays. I hope I am up to say good-bye."

A simple dream, long in the making, crushed in a short conversation. His daddy was right, "Life is a hell of a thing to go through."

Amid it all, Alex fell asleep, free to dream about oranges and baby gators.

In the middle of the night, Alex awoke to the sounds of movement and anger. With the fast squeak of the door, his mama and daddy were in the room. Amy was with them, looking sleepy.

"Get up, put your clothes on, we are getting out of here. I will tell you all about it later," Sandra said.

Uncle Bill stood in the living room doing his best to explain the food under the bed. Aunt Peggy showed no emotion as the family walked past, not even a good-bye.

"Come on, Sandra, get into the car," Robert pleaded.

"No, I have something else to say. Of all the gall, saving the food for the church pantry, my ass."

Sandra turned back toward the house. She began yelling. Her arms moved, as if in sync, with the cuss words she was using. Alex's Aunt and Uncle stood there, in the doorway, staring.

His mother came back to the car, mad as a wet setting hen. Everyone wanted to know why?

"Your mama dropped one of her earrings."

"Let me tell it," Sandra said, "I had to get on my knees to find it and guess what I found?"

"What mama?" Alex said.

"Groceries, they hid all the food under the bed."

"Why would they do that?"

"Because they were too cheap to feed us, that's why. We will never go back."

"I told your daddy we had no business coming down here, as usual, he didn't listen."

There was no money for a place to stay. It was the next day before Alex could sleep in his bed. He was glad to be home with Buster.

Alex figured not moving was for the best, his daddy belonged here on this land, to plow, to plant, to be a farmer.

The school year was almost over. Another day, Alex thought, getting off the bus. He raced to beat his brothers to the kitchen, to the plate of biscuits in the pie safe. With the push and twist of a finger, he poked a hole into the center of one and filled it with cane syrup.

The wind dies down in the afternoon. A perfect time to burn off a field of old corn stalks. Alex grabbed a ragged pair of blue jeans and hurried to join his brothers. He was fascinated by the popping of the fire, and embers floating into the evening sky. In a few days, Frank would plow under the smutty remains of last years crop.

The Morgans lived in a region called the 'Blackbelt of the South'. It was good dirt, rich dirt, and Alex enjoyed walking in it.

Some called the timid birds that followed the tractor, Killdees, others said, Killdeers. They came each year filling their bellies with worms and such.

"I still say they look like seagulls."

"They are not seagulls," Norman said, "It is not like they were hanging out at the beach and decided it was time to fly up to see the Morgans. They are here all the time, hiding in the field grass and hedgerows."

Norman might be right. They showed up pretty fast. Landing in a nervous fit they hurried along the fresh dirt on skinny legs. White feathers fluffed beneath their wings as the breeze hurried them along to another spot, another worm.

Alex stumbled upon another arrowhead on top of the ground. It reminded him of his great-grandmother, a full-blooded Cherokee. Because the Morgan ancestors were mixed in blood with the Cherokee, they were not taken on the 'Trail of Tears'. They were left behind to work the land.

The tilling and planting marked a new beginning. According to the Farmer's Almanac, it would be a hot and dry summer. The only cooling was from the window fans, one in each room. Even being older now, Alex went without his shirt most of the time.

People worked for three dollars a day. Cropping tobacco, a dollar more. Gathering peas paid twenty-five cents, butter-beans fifty-cents a hamper.

The low wages affected blacks more than anyone else. There was no welfare to speak of, not during the summer months, not in Georgia. With no store to issue them credit, it was work or starve.

Schools closed during the summer. The economy depended on the children to help parents and neighbors during the gathering season. Kids wanted to work. It was a way of earning money for next years school clothes and supplies.

One year, Alex had a reason to take a day to enjoy himself. He was in the bedroom, getting ready.

"What are you doing?" Frank said.

"You know, I told you about my class trip. I am going to Steven Foster tomorrow."

"I need you to help me."

"They are your squash, not daddy's. Besides, a boy in my class is coming over here on his daddy's tractor. We are going to give him a ride.

"Come on, just tell him you forgot, he can get someone at the store to take him."

"I will pay you well. You won't be sorry."

The next morning his friend arrived on time. He parked his tractor under a pecan tree and walked the short distance to meet Alex.

"What are you doing picking squash? Did you forget? We have a picnic. Don't you want to see the Suwannee River?"

"I'm sorry, it must have slipped my mind. I'm sure Mr. Baker would be glad to take you to the schoolhouse."

The look on his face said it all. There was nothing Alex could say to make it any better, any worse.

It was a bad thing that I have done, mama and daddy could have stopped it, Alex thought as he shuffled his feet down a row of crooked neck squash. A five-gallon bucket in one hand, and picking squash with the other. Hair like pins pricked his fingers. They are out to get me. I hate helping Frank.

At the Framers Market, Frank got three-fifty a hamper. Afterward, he took Norman and Alex to the Dairy Queen. Alex got a twenty-nine cent chocolate malt, his pay for the day. He didn't know what he gave Norman.

CHAPTER 6

*A*lex liked the washing machine, it was an old wringer type that sat on the back porch. He wondered how his mama ever did without it.

"It does it all, don't it mama?"

"Well, that depends on how you look at it? It is better than a tub and washboard."

"The water sure is dirty. Are you sure the bucket didn't touch the bottom?"

"No, ma'am. I stayed away from the mud."

"I guess we will have to get someone to clean it out?"

"What about the catfish?"

"What catfish?"

"The ones that Norman put in the well to eat the wiggle tails."

"He's too stubborn for his own good. I told him it was not a good idea."

The well-digger wanted to do it on a Sunday. Sandra didn't like Joe Lee, but she agreed. She hoped that God would understand.

Stores closed on Sundays, not always by choice. It was the law. However, even church people liked to shop, so the law changed. It allowed the stores to open at one o'clock.

Frank wanted to clean the well, but his daddy was against it. He said you would have to be crazy or drunk to go down a hole thirty-foot deep. Alex figured his daddy was half-right.

Joe Lee was a man of low reputation, his only friend, the distilled liquor in a clear pint jar. He lived on the Anderson place, in a barn. In exchange, he did a few chores now and again. After a few drinks, he was the best well-digger in the county.

Sandra complained about Joe Lee, the way he dressed, as well as the foul language he used. Robert reminded her, preachers don't dig wells.

Norman and Frank took turns emptying the remaining water out of the well. The pulley squeaked against the fill of the bucket. All that remained was a few feet of muddy water.

Joe Lee showed up as promised. His small frame carried a pick and a shovel, both with handles cut short.

"Y'all about done?"

"Just about," Robert said

Joe Lee wore a pair of ragged jeans and a cut off tee shirt. He was nasty enough to get into a well.

"How much do you think it will cost?"

"Ten dollars, cleaning and digging it down a bit."

"What happened to your little toe?"

"Chopped it off with an axe."

"Alex, leave him alone."

"That's a lot of money for a few hours work?"

"Doing it yourself might cost more than that."

"How you figure?"

"I'll charge your wife twenty dollars to dig you out."

"How long will it take… I mean to clean out the well?"

"Three hours, unless I run into trouble."

"You aren't scared?"

"Get out of the way and let the man work."

Joe Lee double-checked the rope tied around his waist and climbed over the railing. He used holes carved into the clay sides to support his weight. Robert sent the tools down in a lard can with a haywire handle.

One slip of the rope, whether it be tools or buckets of mud, Joe Lee could be killed. Everything went as planned, until Joe Lee yelled.

"Something is moving down here."

"It's just catfish, Norman did it," Alex said, his voice straining to be heard.

"Good God, I thought it was a mud snake."

It took longer than expected. Robert pulled

Joe Lee up twice for fresh air and a cigarette. Mud, water and sweat, he was caked in all of three. He went down again. About a half hour later, he yelled at Robert.

"I hit a good spring. Quick, pull up the toos hurry, the water is rising."

Robert wasted no time in getting the tools out of the way. Joe Lee secured a rope around his waist and shouted for Robert to pull him out of the well.

His feet, muddy from the dig, were unable to grab the climbing holes. The rope went slack as he fell back into the water.

"Joe Lee, are you all right?" Robert shouted.

Alex left to get his mama. She would know what to do.

"Joe Lee, in the well!"

"I'm coming, dear God, don't let it be a cave-in."

Norman, crying, ran to meet his mother.

"I think he is dead, mama."

"Hush, don't talk like that."

Robert stood there, shaking. His face distorted with fear.

"What happened, is he hurt?"

"He won't answer. The rope, I couldn't hold on to the rope."

Sandra told Frank to take the pickup and get Ramon. He lived close by, next to the store. Not a real doctor. However, folks went to him with their ailments.

Frank was back in no time. Ramon got out of the truck and ran to the side of the well.

"Has he moved any? Is he talking?

"He is moving. I can hear him moaning. Can't see much, the flashlight is too dim."

"Let me go down, I can secure him to the rope," Frank said.

In minutes Frank was at the bottom."He's talking. I got the rope under his arms."

Frank was pulled to the top first. Soon, Joe Lee was stretched out on the ground, yelling and moving about.

"Leave me alone. I got to clean the well."

"He needs a town doctor, there's nothing I can do," Ramon said.

Sandra had just finished washing some of the mud off Joe Lee when the sheriff arrived.

"The boys up at the store didn't lie. It looks like you got trouble, all right."

"You ain't taking me back to jail."

"He's been talking out of his head. He needs to go to the hospital," Robert said.

"Don't look at me. I don't want that mud in my car. Why don't you throw him in the back of your truck?"

"Cause it has a bad tire. What if we clean him

up some more and put his other pants on?"

By the time they got him into the patrol car, Joe Lee was talking a little better.

"Don't worry. I've seen things like this before. He's going to be fine."

Night came, still no word about Joe Lee. Sandra went through the motions of fixing supper. More than once, she talked about it being all her fault.

She was the only one that said much about what had happened. The family gathered at the table, the same as the night before.

Sandra said grace, stopping before the amen.

"Stop crying, there is no need to be upset. It was an accident," Robert said.

"I should not have let you talk me into it."

"It's nobody's fault...The fish are good."

"The fish are good, that's all you can say? I bet you wish he would die so you won't have to pay him the ten dollars."

"I should have let Frank do it," Robert said.

"What a terrible thing to say, it could have been your son in the hospital."

It took a few days for the water to clear up. Not only was the mud gone, so were the mosquito offspring. Alex never acquired a taste for wiggle tales.

The preacher told Sandra the hospital refused to treat Joe Lee. Said, the sheriff took him back home, to the Anderson place, and that he was some better.

After more nagging from Sandra, Robert carried Joe Lee his money.

He was wearing nothing but his undershorts when he answered the door for Alex's daddy.

"What you want?"

"It's me, Robert. Are you all right? I brought you your money."

He told Sandra that Joe Lee had nothing much to say. "I don't think he recognized me."

"You should have gone over there before now."

"I should have done a lot of things?" Robert said.

That was the way it was. It was true, Sandra never seemed satisfied, not when it came to Robert.

Not telling Alex what his great idea was, Norman fired up the tractor. He drove around by the side of the barn and backed up to the empty tobacco sled.

"Hook me up, I'm going to take you for a ride. With the rain we had last night, it's got to be muddy down at the bottom corner."

"OK," Alex said, with a grin, jumping into the sled.

Norman pulled out of the yard, and down by the tobacco patch. The stalks were stripped now, except for a few remaining suckers and a worm or two. The 8N Ford purred along for a while until Norman snatched it into high gear.

"Get down and hold on, we are almost there."

Sliding around the curve was nothing new to Alex. However, instead of slowing down, Norman pulled the speed handle to its max. Alex grabbed the burlap sacks, keeping his fingers inside. He felt the sled lean.

"Watch out, it's turning over," Norman yelled.

The sled was on its side, sliding through the mud. Alex held tight until it came to a stop.

"Alex, are you all right?"

"You did have a good idea."

"You weren't scared?

"Of course, not."

"Are you sure I didn't scare you?"

Alex shook his head.

"I see," Norman said, "I guess we might as well be heading back."

My brothers keep trying, but I am brave and not afraid.

Robert was waiting at the barn.

"Norman what on earth are you doing?"

"Alex wanted me to pull him around in the sled."

"Get out Alex. Norman put up the tractor. Y'all meet me on the porch."

Daddy is going to beat me. He always whips me on the porch.

Alex and Norman were slow getting to the house. Robert was waiting, a limb in his hand.

Norman was the first to get it. Alex hoped his whipping would be as quick.

"Alex come on over here, boy, you know better than to cause trouble."

"Norman asked me?"

"It don't make any difference." He grabbed Alex by his left arm and began switching his behind. The one thing that Alex did to make his daddy mad was to act like it didn't bother him.

"Hold still and stop that singing."

Robert hit him with greater force, lowering the switch to the back of Alex's knees.

One day, daddy won't hurt me no more.

Norman had one friend, a redheaded boy, named Clarence. Unlike Norman, he was old enough to drive. He came by one Sunday afternoon.

He was quick to ask Norman if he was ready to go.

"How about me, I want to go?" Alex said.

"It's a long walk."

"You're not taking the car?"

"Do you want to go or not?"

Alex followed as they walked into the woods behind the house. Three miles later, they reached the road at Five Forks.

"Where are we going?"

"To that house across the road. Clarence has already checked the place out."

"The house is empty, I saw some things in the barn," Clarence said.

"We shouldn't be doing this, what if we get caught?"

"Come on," Norman said.

Clarence took an English riding saddle. Norman got a lawn mower.

"What do you want, Alex?"

"Nothing, I'm not getting into trouble."

"You already are, you better take something. Here, since you are such a good boy, how about a cross?"

It was a plastic cross, more pink than red. On it hung a statue, a silver-plated Jesus. Alex took it, with no thought of what to do with it. They ran back across the road and into the woods.

Once they got back to the shed, Clarence left the side-saddle, it was made for a girl, and besides, he didn't even have a horse. Later, Alex threw it and the cross into the weeds along the ditch bank.

Norman kept the mower, a little green thing, not more than two horsepower. Robert heard the sputtering and walked up as Norman tried to keep it running.

"Where did you get it, son?"

"From Clarence, his granddaddy gave it to him. I thought I would fix it up."

"You know his family is nothing but white trash. I don't want him coming around."

Alex hoped no one would ever find the saddle and pink cross. If so, he would tell his mama the truth.

They were not separate, good and evil, not the way he once thought. The house wasn't empty. He knew it was a lie. There were curtains on the windows. Alex had no intention of staying, taking the silver Jesus, but he did.

TED VICK

CHAPTER 7

*T*here was a flaw in his family that others did not see. Alex saw it, heard it, he could even smell it. It came in the middle of the night, to torment him, making him put aside his dreams and face reality.

Unwelcome voices, familiar and strange, they came from the next room and entered his mind. Faint at first and then louder and moving about the house. It was always the same, the conflict between his parents. Their talk filled with foulness, the only time Alex ever heard them cuss, except for that time in Florida.

"The Five and Dime should not be selling that filth. Life is not a picnic, not some romantic story in a magazine," Robert said.

"I know you are tired at night," Sandra said, "but It would be nice, if sometimes...? I just want you to spend time with me, that's all."

"And when do you think I have any time, it's hard enough as it is?"

"That's the point it isn't hard enough."

"You are talking like a slut. Maybe Tom Atkins can help you out? I know that is what you would like."

"Robert, you are wrong, I have always been faithful to you."

There was too much movement, and cussing, it had been going on for hours. Frank and Norman stayed in bed, they had heard worse. What was daddy doing to mama? He cracked the door of his bedroom to see.

They were in the hallway. Alex could smell the sweat and the blood in the heat of the night, the fight. It was spotted, the blood on his daddy's undershirt and boxer shorts. His mama's face looked swollen but not scratched. Too tired to fight any longer, Sandra grabbed Robert's undershirt and fell to her knees.

"Please, I'm begging you. I want you to love me. Please tell me you love me? I cannot go on like this anymore."

Her hands fell down beside her. Robert left her there, slumped to the floor, sobbing. Sandra wanted one thing from Robert. However, not only did he not give her what she desired, he couldn't even say the words.

Alex closed the door, but the image remained, his mother there on the floor. Daddy should have said he loved her. That he loved me.

Sadness followed Alex as he walked past the empty fields of cotton. They reminded him of Ester. Alex had heard she wasn't doing well. He did not know if she was ill in the way some medicine could heal. Or, if she was sick of all the pain, tired of the struggle she had endured.

Should he dare to ask his mama to pray for Ester? What if, she asked God to let her live when Ester's last hope might be the hope for it all to end?

Ester would not go to a real doctor. She had no use for them, not since they came and took her husband away. The doctor and a deputy sheriff, came wearing masks over their faces, she said.

She begged them to leave him alone. They said it was the law. They tried to assure Ester that he would be better off in the sanatorium. She knew it was not the truth. Her husband, weak from coughing, could not stop them. They put handcuffs on him and escorted him to the patrol car.

He was supposed to be back in a few months. He wasn't. The last time Ester saw her husband was that day, slumped over in the back seat, disappearing into a cloud of dust.

After all the years, Ester would only go to a root doctor. She never went anywhere without her necklace of potion. Daddy said most blacks are superstitious.

The days were getting shorter. Firewood was chopped and stacked on the porch. The sun dropped low in the sky as smoke curled from the chimney. The washtub was emptied and hung on the side of the house. There would be no baths until next year, not outside.

They had enough money, but none to waste. It had to last until spring. Sandra put up canned goods, and there were plenty of preserves. The hard work of summer eased into the slow pace of fall.

Sandra started writing again, short stories of places she had not known. Late into the night, she stayed, at the table, with her paper, and her dreams.

The fireplace was the only heat. As a family not used to staying in the same room, they talked and moved around a lot. It was hard to keep warm, harder still to be civil to one another. With no habit of kindness, Alex was quick to aggravate Amy.

"You're fat."

"I am not."

"Yes, you are, ask daddy."

"You could lose a few pounds," Robert said.

She could not hide her disappointment. Later, she cried. Robert had to say he was sorry.

Bedtime came early, Alex had not wet the bed in years unless he ate watermelon. Regardless, his brothers refused to sleep with him.

The bedroom door was left part way. From his bed, Alex could see the fireplace, the oak logs, alive with the glow of red embers. They were quick to fade into the night. Would he go the same way? He pulled the quilted blankets around him, afraid to close his eyes.

The next day, Alex was shucking corn for the chickens. His mother came and stood at the crib door. She looked younger, and for a change, alive and full of energy. Her brown eyes sparkled against a face absent of any wrinkles, her lips red in color, each smile filled with love and contentment. In her hand was a letter, ripped at the fold. She had sold a story to some people in, New York.

It contained a five-hundred-dollar check. She had a right to be proud of what she had done. Before leaving, she said, "Don't tell your daddy."

Perhaps she thought his daddy would feel less of a man if he saw her check, the first one she ever had.

He did seem sad and unsettled, moving about from the bed to the couch. Unable to sleep, losing weight. He appeared lost in thought, not being able to figure out what to do.

 It was Ester's last winter in the cold house

with the tin and tar paper roof. In the end, she just stopped, like a broken watch. Alex was glad she was free from her long illness and the pain it had caused.

On the day of the funeral, a Christmas wreath hung on the door of the church. Her people said she liked bright and happy colors.

June Bug invited Alex to the service. It might not have been proper, for a twelve-year-old, white boy, to go to the funeral, but Alex liked Ester. He did not ask his daddy. Alex figured he was old enough to make up his own mind.

Blue jeans and a clean shirt were the best clothes he had. Most of the people were already inside the church. As Alex entered the front door, he saw Levi, sitting on the back row, next to the wall. There was just enough space left for Alex.

June Bug stood for a moment next to the casket of simple pine boards, hand-planed smooth. Alex was glad that it was closed. Green jasmine with white flowers draped over the top and down the front side. The church was filled with its sweetness.

All her people said Ester was in a better place. The songs they sang were different, more upbeat than the Church of God. Moving to the beat of the piano, clapping and singing, carrying on like nothing Alex had ever seen.

Dressed in a white suit, the preacher had class. He stood tall and confident, with a voice so compelling, dare say, he could resurrect a sinner from the pits of hell and have him sitting next to God in the stroke of a few words.

"Be like Ester," he shouted, "She praised God all the time. It made no difference if she was picking the white man's cotton or in the pew, Ester never lost her faith in God."

They sang another hymn. The preacher started up again. Alex could picture Ester climbing that mountain, he talked about. Never giving up, even when her friends said it was no use, she kept on climbing. He ended his hour-long sermon with Ester on the top of that mountain shouting, "God is good. God is good all the time."

As they sang Swing Low, Sweet Chariot Alex imagined, that this church of old boards and white paint was also swaying. With its steeple pointed toward heaven, saying, 'Swing Low Sweet Chariot,' Ester is ready to go home.

Ester traded her dull-colored dress for a long flowing gown. And in her hand, once where cotton stayed, now held flowers that God had made.

TED VICK

CHAPTER 8

*L*ife keeps ongoing. It never stops when someone dies. Ester was gone, no one spoke of her anymore. Like embers in a fireplace, she faded into the night. Alex had a lot of learning to do, about death, about life. Some of his lessons were about to unfold.

Despite what his daddy had said, Norman was still hanging out with Clarence. One morning, on a Friday he pulled into the yard. Norman hurried to meet him.

"Norman where are you going?"

"To see a man about a dog."

"You always say that to me."

"You can come along if you promise not to get scared?"

They traveled a good ten miles before Clarence parked the car.

"This is it," Clarence said, "Mr. Potter's place is across the field."

"How long y'all been sharecroppers?" Norman asked.

"Ever since daddy got laid off at the factory."

They walked along the hedgerow, and into a stand of pines. I few hundred yards away was a pigpen, next to a large pond.

"Any fish in it?" Alex said.

"Last year I caught a five-pound bass."

After about ten minutes, they spotted Mr. Potter in his pickup.

"I told you, same time every day."

"Shoo-wee, so-wee," he yelled, shucking the ears of corn, before throwing them into the pen.

"Alex, when he leaves I want you to go down next to the dam. If he comes back, wave your hands and hide in the woods."

"What if he sees me?"

"He's not going to, as long as you do your job right."

Alex did as they said. Before long, a pig squealed. He looked back to see a pig with a rope around his neck. By the time he got to the pen, they were already gone. Alex caught up with them at the hedgerow.

"What took you so long? We thought old man Potter had caught you."

Norman joked, "Instead of a pig in a blanket, we have a pig on a rope."

Alex did not see the humor in it.

"Daddy will want to know where you got it.

"The pig is not for us, stupid."

"We are taking him to the slaughterhouse."

"It's just a little pig, let me take him back?"

"Stop whining."

At the road, Clarence pulled on the fence, making an opening large enough for the pig.

He stopped squealing after he was stuffed into the trunk. From the back seat, Alex heard him gasping for air.

When they reached the packing house, Alex and Norman waited in the car.

"He is taking too long. I hope we are not in trouble," Norman said.

Clarence walked out of the office with two black men.

"They gotta weigh him up."

"The deed was done. Did they say anything about us having a pig in a car?"

"Oh, yeah, so I made up a story about the truck, not cranking."

"How much?" Norman said, reaching out his hand.

"Here, five for you and five for me."

Thirty pieces of silver. "You shouldn't have sold the pig. They are going to kill him."

"What about the pig? Shut up about the pig?"

Until his mind filled with some other worry, Alex could not stop thinking about the pig.

Stock car racing and red-necks went together like peanut butter and jelly. It was Saturday afternoon, Alex and his brothers scraped up just enough money for tickets to the last race of the season.

It was a forty-mile trip to the Valdosta Speedway. Alex was surprised when Frank stopped to get a six-pack.

"What are you doing, you know we don't have the money?" Alex said.

"Stop your whining. I got everything under control."

The race had already started by the time they arrived. Dust clouded the air as cars without mufflers sped around the dirt track. They roared like lions in the night air. They were in luck, or perhaps fate had reserved them a parking space near the front entrance.

"I'll buy the tickets. Y'all meet me at the chain-link fence," Frank said.

He came back with his ticket and handed it through the fence to Norman.

"Stay here, Alex. Norman will give you his ticket in a minute."

Alex should have known better than to think Frank had put back any extra money.

Before the final lap, Frank said it was time to

leave. In the bed of the pickup, parked next to them, was a case of drinks. "Y'all want some cokes?" Not waiting for an answer, Frank picked them up.

Norman spotted a motorcycle parked over near a wall.

"That is a pretty bike."

"You want it? Let's get it," Frank said.

The race was over, people were coming out of the gate. "I'm going," Alex said.

He walked fast out to the dirt road, then headed toward the highway. His brothers caught up with him.

"Get in," Norman yelled as he opened the door.

"No. I'm walking home."

"You going to get us caught. It will only be a few minutes before it's reported stolen," Frank said.

"Get your butt in the truck, now! Norman said, jumping out, grabbing Alex, forcing him into the front seat.

It seemed longer than it was, but now, the city was left behind. We made it. We will be home before long. The hum of tires on hard-gravel echoed against the tall pines, for a while it was the only sound.

Frank saw lights in the rearview mirror, "They are coming fast. If we get caught, I'll take all the blame."

Streaks of blue light, they were caught. Why

was Frank not slowing down?

"Give me a dirt road. Please, God, give me a dirt road?"

What was he going to do with a dirt road? Alex had seen things like this in the movies. The police are going to start shooting.

With a bump of the siren, the officer gave Frank one last chance to pull over. We are going to go to jail.

"Both of you shut up, let me do all the talking."

The officer got out of his car. He shined his flashlight over the motorcycle and then again before it stopped upon their faces.

"What are you boys up to, this time of night?"

"Nothing, just going home from the races."

"Is that your bike?"

"Yes, sir," Frank said.

"Can I see your driver's license?"

He stared at it for a moment before ordering Frank to step out of the truck."

Frank got out and followed the officer to the tailgate.

"Are you any kin to Mr. Ralph Morgan?"

"He is my granddaddy."

"Let me be clear, you not stopping, I didn't take kind to it," the officer hesitated, "I have a mind to throw the whole bunch of you in jail. You have a tail light out. You need to get that fixed."

"Yes, sir."

"Y'all boys drive careful. Next time you see your granddaddy tell him, officer Joe Freeman said, hello."

"Yes, sir. Thank you, sir."

Once the patrol car was out of sight, Frank started his bragging.

"Did you see how I talked him out of putting us in jail? Norman, what kind of story are you going to tell daddy?"

"I will figure it out later. In the meantime, we can hide the bike over at granddaddy's pecan orchard. The house is empty. He never goes there anymore."

There he was, after four years, in the same truck, in front of their home. The 'skinny man' was back.

"Sam, we must have made you mad? Where you been?" Robert asked.

"Near Fargo, down at the Okefenokee. My sister took ill. Stayed there until she died."

"You moving back?"

"Yes, sir. In the same old house as before. No one wants to live there, except me. Mr. Simmons was glad to see me."

"How are you, Alex? I got you some candy."

"No, sir."

"Since when? Take it, you never get too old for candy. Here, I got enough for you and your sister."

Robert bought a can of Prince Albert rolling tobacco and some lard.

Frank said later, "Sam was lying about ever being from New Orleans. He is nothing more than a Georgia, swamp boy."

Alex gave Amy all of the candy with a plea for her to never talk to Sam alone.

Maybe, Alex was exaggerating about what had happened on the dirt road. Perhaps Sam would not hurt them, but he was determined not to take that chance.

"Alex come in here. I want to talk to you."

"Since when do you say 'Sir' to a black man?"

"It just slipped out."

"Slipped out? I better never hear you do it again. He is uppity enough as it is."

His daddy was right. Alex hoped Sam would remember the white sheets and hooded faces of the past. No one talked about it much, but someone had to keep people in their place. This included wife beaters and such, be it black or white.

The last reported lynching in the county was in 1936. The only unsolved crime was up around Pebble City. A little girl went missing, no one ever found out what happened to her.

No matter what his daddy said about calling a black, Sir, he would never disrespect Levi. He was not like the rest of his people.

Today would be the first time going to Levi's on the bicycle. Levi was on the porch steps, sharping a hoe. I wonder where Boo is?

"Mr. Morgan, It has been a while. You got you a new set of wheels."

"Yes, sir, it is Norman's old bike."

"I thought you had forgotten about me? What have you been up to?"

"Trying to keep Norman out of trouble, that's why he gave me the bike."

"Where is Boo?"

"She got bit by a rattler."

"Did she die?"

"No Sir, it's hard to kill a good dog like Boo. In the last few days, the swelling in her leg has gone down. She will be stove up for a week or two."

"She is under the porch, around next to the fig tree. I figured it would be cooler there."

She was still and only opened her eyes when Alex touched her. She groaned as Alex stroked her with his hand.

"She is real sick? I will ask mama to pray for her. It will be all right, Boo. I will come back to see you tomorrow. Your daddy is going to take care of you."

Before leaving, he told Levi about Sam.

"The last I heard he was up around Albany, but that was a while back. You can hear almost anything. It is hard to tell a lie from the truth these days. Something bad must have happened for him to go back to Fargo, to the swamp. I didn't know he had a sister."

"Sam is evil, I know he is," Alex said.

"It is a bad thing to be cursed. Best for us to leave the spirits be."

CHAPTER 9

If prayers were raindrops, the Morgans would have had plenty of rain that year. Sometimes things are the way they are, and no amount of wishing and praying will make it any better. Hard times fall on good people. Some just take it better than others.

The one person seemed to fair better than most was the insurance man. He came by the same time, each month,

"Jim, I know you must be hurting along with the rest of us?" Robert said.

"Not as much as you would think."

"Come on, it is hard enough for me to pay you?" The blacks have to be hiding from you.

"No, not at all. You know how suspicious they are. All I do is tell them I had a dream about them. I go on with the story of how they were fine one minute and dead the next."

"It works. You can get just about anything you want. All you have to do is tell a good enough story.

It didn't make any sense to Alex, it was called life insurance when the only way to get the money was to die, and you didn't get it then.

His daddy told Sandra that he was worth more dead than alive. She told him he was scaring the children with such foolish talk.

A few weeks later, Alex saw his daddy with the shotgun.

"Where are you off to?" Alex said.

"To the other side of the crib, I saw a rat I want to shoot."

"I will go with you,"

"Don't worry about me. I will be back before long. Why don't you go back to the house, your mother could use some help."

I should have insisted on going with him. Alex waited, then the sound of a shot. Alex found him behind the barn. He got there just in time to see his daddy throw a dead waif rat into the bushes.

"What is the matter, son? Don't tell me you are scared of a little rat?"

He was not the best father in the world, but that did not stop Alex from worrying about him. His daddy suffered too much. Once, he found him in the kitchen with his head in the oven. He said he was desperate. He thought the heat might help. It didn't.

After that, Alex had nightmares of his daddy's

head, baking over a pile of bay leaves. He never forgot the smell. One night daddy begged me to shoot him in the head with the twelve-gauge. It seemed too real to be a dream.

Alex needed time to be alone, time to think about something else. He was eager to try his new rifle scope. All the hunters in the Field and Stream magazine had rifle scopes.

Down the road, lived a mean sort of a man, made his living as a chain gang guard. Alex had permission to hunt on his land. A short man, he was, with a stern face and most often seen with a string of chew-tobacco running out the corner of his mouth. Always ready for a fight, a thirty-eight strapped to his side.

Mr. Howard was a walking boss, best known as the man with no heart. He stopped by once in a while to chew the fat with Robert.

"Whites or blacks, that sling blade don't know there is a difference, the roadway gets cleared just the same. Biscuits and syrup, for breakfast and lunch, and a plate of beans for supper, that's all they get."

"You ever have any go off?

"No, not many. I tell them, if you run, I'm going to kill you."

"I shot two, both of them black. Ain't seen nobody yet that could outrun a twelve-gauge slug."

"Did it bother you?"

"If they won't listen, there is nothing else to do.
I shot both of them through the heart. Bother me?
Not in the least."

If Mr. Howard had a kind side, it didn't show.
He wasn't doing Alex a favor, the squirrels were eating his corn.

Alex entered the woods by way of a small
creek. The running water was down to a trickle,
giving him plenty of room to walk on its sandy bed
into the swamp.

It was darker, beneath the canopy of trees. In
the distance, the sound of chatter and three squirrels playing. They scattered when Alex, in his excitement, stepped on a twig.

Alex spotted the one that was left behind near
the very top of the tree clinging to a branch, afraid
to move. If he had no scope, the squirrel would be
safe to run and play another day.

He leaned against a sweet gum and braced
his rifle. He took a deep breath, his finger pulled
against the flat iron of the trigger.

The bullet exploded with the sound of death
as it raced toward the kill. There was a falling, thirty
feet or more, from the top of the live oak, down to

the water-filled ground. A splash signaled the end of life.

The squirrel landed in knee-deep water. His front legs moved to stay afloat. He struggled to reach the trunk of the tree to feel the bark beneath his feet, one more time. Before with birds and such, it was not like this, they died without a whimper.

He looked smaller now, I picked him up, so wet, so scared. Beneath my hands, I felt the beat of his heart. His back legs paralyzed from the glance of the bullet against his spine. I had to bring to a close what I had started, there was no turning back. He was too close to death, and no amount of wishing and praying could put him back together. How could I have done this?

There was no way Alex was going to eat him. The little squirrel deserved better. He carried him to the creek bank. There, with his hands, he dug a grave. As he covered him with sand and tears, he thought about Bambi. At that moment he realized, he was 'the man in the woods.'

Alex started the day with his jacket. It now lay to the side, it was a perfect day in November to gather sweet potatoes. Of all the crops, Alex liked, he liked this one the best.

Frank grabbed the 8n Ford. He was smiling as he lowered the bottom plow into the dirt. He set it deep, and with slow speed, he turned the potatoes to the top of the ground. Alex and Norman brushed the dirt off and placed them in baskets for the short ride to a place closer to the house.

They are safe now, Alex thought, as Norman shoved the last bit of dirt on top of the bed of straw and taters.

Before going back to the house, Norman told Alex he overheard their mother say something about going to the hospital.

"I don't believe you, she is not sick."

"Well someone must be going to the hospital."

"It can't be mama," Alex said.

Alex was right, he found out that it was his daddy that needed to go. Alex felt guilty for being happy that it wasn't his mama.

His daddy's stomach was giving him trouble. It had been going on for a long time. He found out that it was an ulcer.

Although Robert refused to go, Sandra kept on about it.

"We do not have the money, and I still owe the bank. What if I don't make it?"

"Sure, you will make it. Dr. Johnson said it was a common operation. They will take out part of your stomach, you will be like new."

"Like new, I am not like new now, we are not like new," Robert said.

"There is one thing...I was talking to Mrs. Baker," Sandra said.

"That witch. What were you doing talking to her? None of this is any of her business."

"She was just trying to help. She said something like this happened to her cousin. However, the man's heart stopped. There was nothing the doctors could do."

"Thanks for trying to cheer me up."

"The point is, the bank was holding the note on their house. She was forced to move out. I am just thinking about the children."

"The bank holds the title on last year's loan. I can't change it now."

"Yes, you can. The bank sent it back the first of this year. It is in the dresser with the rest of our paper-work."

"It has to be a mistake. Why didn't you tell me?"

"It came the same week that Norman was in all of that trouble. I was going to tell you, it just slipped my mind. It is the bank's loss."

"I don't know if it would be legal. What did the letter say, there had to be a letter with it."

"Nothing, except, *Enclosed is your security deed. We appreciate your business.*"

Frank knew the farm would never be his, not if his mother got her hands on it. Alex heard Frank tell Robert their mama could not be trusted. It went on like that for about a week.

By the look on Frank's face, Alex knew that his daddy was going to go ahead with it. They had the paper work notarized in Pavo.

Robert said when the bank finds out about it, he will have hell to pay.

CHAPTER 10

*A*lex spent the next day hanging around the shed with Norman. Coming up the road, past the place where Alex had hidden the saddle and cross, walked a lean frame of a boy. He had no hurry out him, to one side of the road or to the other. He stopped at the edge of the yard,

"Someone is here," Alex said.

"I see him, stay here, I will do the talking."

Not wanting the boy to get too close, Norman hurried to meet him.

"What you want?"

"Some work if I…"

"There is no work here, you best go on."

Norman waited for him to get down the road a piece before turning back around to Alex.

"Do you think he saw anything?

"I don't think so,"

"You got to watch them, you know they will steal you blind."

A few months later, Frank and Alex saw the

same boy hanging around the store.

"I heard you needed work," Frank said.

"Yes, sir."

"Where are you from?"

"Sally May's, I am her nephew, they call me Willie."

"I think I can use you on Saturday."

"Yes, sir. Thank you, sir."

For all the work that Willie did, Frank only gave him a dollar or two. At times, Willie would work all day for an R. C. Cola and a moon pie. Willie never asked for anything, except for that one time, a bag of potato chips was all he wanted.

Frank did not like it, not one bit. He left for the store, not saying a word. When Frank came back, instead of stopping at the shed, he threw the bag of chips out the truck window.

Willie ran to pick them up, out of the dirt. He was eating them when Frank walked up from the house, Alex behind him.

While Frank was gone, Willie made the mistake of saying, "There was no need for him not to answer me."

"Alex said you were talking about me behind my back. Do you want to repeat it?"

"No Sir, Mr. Frank, I was just kidding, I don't mean nothing by it."

Frank kept an old axe handle in one corner of

the shed. He was quick to pick it up. Willie begged Frank not to hit him.

"I tell you what I think I will just be kidding by knocking you in the head."

"No Sir, Mr. Frank, you know I like working here."

"Well…You don't work here anymore, now get your sorry self, off our place."

Before supper, Alex and Frank sat on the porch, in metal chairs, rust spotted green with tube-shaped arms that curved at the end and down toward the wood floor. Frank had his feet propped on one of the brick pillars that held up the square post of the porch.

Willie had come back and was now at the edge of the yard. Then, he stopped for a moment, like a beat dog, pondering what to do, slow to walk toward the house. He eased his way around the outside of the steps, and through the bushes that lined the porch.

He stood shorter than usual, his work pants gathered at the waist and a shirt part way open, a shirt soiled from the grease of motor work beneath the shed. His shoes were hand-me-down big, gaped at the ankles with no socks to fill the space.

Frank sat there like an inconsiderate judge, his feet not leaving the prop of the post. Frank had the look of sternness, with the power to forgive, or not.

"Well…" Frank said, "You learned your lesson?"

Willie dropped his face as if too ashamed to look at Frank. His lips quivered, his voice soft and filled with remorse. Before today, Alex had never seen tears on a face of color.

"Yes, sir."

"I reckon you can go on back to the shed and finish sweeping the floor."

"Yes, sir. Thank you, Mr. Frank."

"Alex, I hope you were paying attention, you never can give them the upper hand."

"Why did you do that to him? You have no feelings for anyone."

"Don't blame me."

Frank was right. It was all my fault. After that, Willie was not the same, he obeyed more than he was polite. Norman and Frank became more demanding, the same as Robert.

Willie withdrew into his place, a place that Frank and all those before him had built. He would stay there for the rest of his life. Like a blind mouse in a box, scurrying around the edge, he too would return to the corner, afraid of any thought of turning left or right.

It is better for Willie to stay in the corner of his world. Where would he go, if he escaped? What would await him in a place he had never known?

His mind might deceive him into thinking he is one of us, and Willie is not. Not now. Perhaps never.

Norman spent a lot of time working on the stolen bike. He changed the serial number and put a fresh coat of paint on it. A notary who was a friend of the family approved the paperwork for a tag. Norman made one mistake, he sold the bike to little Jimmy Baker.

It was on a Saturday, Norman drove up fast, Alex was on the front porch,

"Alex, you got to help me?"

"Now what?"

"The boy that owned the motorcycle saw it at the store. Mr. Baker called the law. They will be here soon to take me to jail. Just, say you were with me that night. I will do the rest."

"Not me, you got the wrong person."

"Do you want to see me locked up?"

"No, but I can't help you, I told you and Frank, y'all would get into trouble."

Just before dark, a sheriff's car pulled into the front yard. Robert went out on the porch to greet them.

"Mr. Morgan, is Norman home?"

"Yes, sir. Norman, come on out here," he

yelled.

"Norman, I am Deputy Barnes, and this is my partner Deputy Cook. Mr. Baker said you sold him that motorcycle. Is that true?"

"Yes, sir."

"Why did you leave in such a hurry?"

"I had something to check on."

"The boy at the store says it is his. Someone had changed the serial number. You might as well tell us. Where did you get it?"

"I was coming home one night, saw a boy on the side of the road with bike trouble. I stopped to help, but we could not get it cranked. He told me he had to get to Florida and needed only enough money for a bus ticket. I had thirty-five dollars, to my surprise, he said I could have the bike. Honest, that's happened."

"I think you stole the bike, but I can't prove it. The owner was glad to get his bike back, I don't think he will press the issue."

"You know he stole the bike," his partner said, "I think we ought to take him to jail."

"This family has a good reputation, best for us to leave it be. Besides, the owner said the bike looked great with the new paint job."

They left with Robert's apologies.

"I have tried to keep you out of trouble. You lie just like your mama, you always have. We don't need the law coming out here, I can hear your granddaddy now."

He forced Norman to work for Mr. Baker until he paid back the money. The last thing, Robert wanted was to lose his account at the store.

Alex never forget that day at the store, the things his father said, the jesters he made.

"I brought my girl with me this morning."

"Say something to Mr. Baker."

Alex looked down, "I don't know anything to say."

"Now tell me? What kind of talk is that? The boy went to bed, and this is what I got this morning? We have already nicknamed him, 'The Duck.'"

"Robert, you shouldn't tease the boy like that, our voices changed like that when we were growing up."

"Not like that, I never sounded like that."

"Robert, I got something to ask you?" Mr. Baker said as he motioned for Robert to join him at the end of the counter. Alex moved so he could hear the conversation without being noticed.

"You are embarrassing the boy, you shouldn't talk to him that way."

"If I want to I can, there's no law against it."

"Well... I'm just saying."

"Keep it to yourself."

Daddy stood upright, "Give me a pack of Camels."

Robert turned to Alex, "Come on, Donald, let's go home."

His daddy was that way. If he knew how much it hurt? Would he still call me names?

The next morning, Alex was eager to get on the school bus, away from his father. Alex's classmates were also uncertain about their feelings, other boy's sounded different too.

Unlike the Sixth grade, Alex was excited to have a pretty girl sitting at the desk in front of him. Her name was Jennifer. The rays of sunlight through the glass panes made her hair sparkle. Like strands of gold, her hair fell across her shoulders, stopping short of Alex's desktop. It seemed to say, feel my softness.

"Stop it."

"I was just touching it."

She resisted the touch, but with a smile. It confused Alex, his daddy said women could do that to a man. However, Alex knew one thing for sure, this girl looked good in a green plaid skirt and white cotton blouse. The buttons were mother-of-pearl and fastened, all except for the top one.

He enjoyed looking, the two buttons closed

tight to the skin, in colors of milk and cream. He wanted to see what was behind them, more than he wanted that baby alligator.

At night his thoughts magnified as he lay in bed, his body on fire with every touch. He dreamed about the girl with golden strands of long hair, blue eyes, and things not seen, only imagined.

The next day, a group of girls stood in the hallway. Jennifer looked better in person than she did in his dream. Alex stopped to talk. She seemed in a good mood, the way she teased and flirted, with her eyes bright, and a blouse too tight.

Those buttons, they stared at Alex as if to say, I dare you. And Alex did, he reached out and touched her right breast. Jennifer seemed stunned and embarrassed.

What have I done? There were no other boys around except for John, his distant cousin.

"Alex, what did you do that for? The principal is going to beat you good."

Alex looked over at the girls again, they were laughing and smiling, only one girl, somewhat homey in appearance was the only one that looked offended.

No one said anything about it, that day, nor the next. If it had not been for his cousin, he might have gotten away with it. Alex could not change John's mind, he would have no part of Alex having all the fun.

He chose the girl with the big breasts, the plain one with no smile. It was not a brush of the hand, a simple soft touch, he right out grabbed her. She looked more than offended. The girls did not laugh, not this time. Alex knew he was in trouble.

The next day the teacher stood before the class. In disbelief, she looked at Alex and his cousin John.

"It has come to my attention, a couple of boys in the room have been messing with my girls. I never imagined such a thing. I will say this one time. This will be the end of such disgusting behavior."

That afternoon, the principal, Mr. Wade, came to the door and called Alex out of the classroom, leaving his classmates to wonder what kind of punishment he would get.

"Alex, you look like you could use a break. Let's walk down to the pottery room."

"I heard your brother got into some trouble the other day?"

"Norman? Yes, sir."

"How is your mama doing?"

"Just fine."

They walked into the room, to a blast of hot air. As Mr. Wade reached to adjust the oven down a notch, he asked Alex about the bowl he had made in the fourth grade.

"I remember, before the oven cooled down,

you wanted to take it out. You were so excited. I see nothing has changed."

Aware of what he meant, Alex looked at the floor.

"Some things are worth waiting for," he said, placing his hand on Alex's shoulder.

"It won't happen again."

"I think we can go back now."

Life is tough, I thought, but it does give you something to hope for.

TED VICK

CHAPTER 11

To touch, to kiss, to hold her, that is all Alex wanted to do with the girl in his class. What was wrong with daddy? Mama is pretty.

Home alone, Alex searched their bedroom and found one magazine hid under the mattress. Titles such as 'Kiss Me' and 'Too Many Men' were on the cover.

There was one story called 'The Farm Girl.' The woman, trapped in a cold relationship reminded him of his mama. The girl also had long black hair and brown eyes. It looked like the marriage would end in tragedy until the night they rekindled their love.

The last few paragraphs described the raw desire of their passion. They held each other close, with whispers of, I love you. His hand moved down and then up again, caressing her breasts.

It had to be his mother's story if so, it was a fantasy. There were no happy endings, not here, in the real world.

Alex was in the hall that night, the night he passed by his mama's bedroom, the door part-way open. He saw her in the dim-lit room, in front of her dresser. Black hair, with the look of silk, flowed past her shoulders and down her back. Her robe was open in the front as she looked into the mirror. Did daddy see her beauty, feel her passion?

She was all woman as she stood, silent. However, she was not alone, the demon inside her moved his hands, the same as hers, to the whiteness of her throat. Fingers stretched tight, her face turned red, she closed her eyes as tears overflowed down her cheeks. Did she feel so worthless as to want to squeeze all the evil thoughts from her body?

My mama is not right, not in her head. Why would she punish herself, as if God could not forgive her sins? I wish I were God, to touch, to kiss, and to hold her. To say, I am the fixer of all flawed things. But I can't fix you mama, let alone, myself.

A few days later, Alex asked his mother what was wrong with their family, with her?

"I can't talk about it."

"I'm not little anymore, mama."

"Just the same, it is better if you did not know."

"Baby, it is getting late, I will see you in the morning."

Alex thought it had to do with Norman. He did not remember one good thing that his daddy ever said concerning him. The only love Norman got was from his mother. Not that his daddy liked Norman less, Alex thought he did not like him at all. There was nothing special about him, except maybe, his ability to fix motors and such. Norman stayed to himself, he was not part of the family, perhaps he wasn't.

It was what they did not say, the people in the community. Alex knew they were talking about the once perfect couple, the lovely couple, his parents now, fallen from grace. There was no place to hide, no place to go.

Alex knew things were getting out of hand. Why else would Dr. Johnson want to see him and Frank? Perhaps other people also saw Norman as different. He wasn't invited.

Alex followed Frank into the front room of the clinic. The doctor's wife, also his nurse, asked for them to wait in his office. Alex had pictured his office with leather chairs and a desk cluttered with medical books. However, It was nothing more than a table in the corner of a small room with just enough room for a few books and a note pad.

In a few minutes, Dr. Johnson walked in, dressed more like a man off the street than that of a real doctor. He was a little overweight and had a gruff sounding voice, not at all the kind that would put a person at ease.

Without much of a greeting, he took a seat. His large frame and burly arms made the table look even smaller.

"I need to talk with y'all about your daddy. As you must know, things have not been going well. I am sorry, and I hate to say it, but there is no hope left for them to get any better. There is not much I can do to help him, not anymore.

"Is he that sick?" Frank said.

"No, and yes, he does not have headaches, not the migraines he talks about. They are only in his mind. If I don't give him shots, he might hurt himself. He can't do without them."

"Frank, I want you to leave home now, and Alex as soon as you get old enough you should do the same. Your mama and daddy... As I said, it will only get worse."

"There has to be something else you could do for daddy?"

"I wish that was the case."

Frank promised to give it some thought. They returned to the truck. Alex asked Frank if he was going to leave?

"Don't you say a word about what happened today. You know he is nothing but a pill-pushing quack. Daddy needs shots because of him. He could get daddy off of them if he wanted to. I am not going anywhere, I'm a farmer just like daddy."

Frank was right, the doctor had given daddy any drug he wanted, anytime, day or night, as long as he could pay. I also knew the doctor was right, It would only get worse.

And it did. Robert threatened to eat poison, to end the misery of his pain in his head and in his life. He said he should have listened to his daddy, he told him not to marry Sandra. "Nothing good comes from marrying a fourteen-year-old girl."

Robert had left in the pickup. Frank and Alex took the car to see if they could find him. The only place they could think to go was to the doctor's office. They traveled past Mr. Bakers store, the car doing well over a hundred miles an hour. The clinic and their daddy's truck were insight in a matter of three or four minutes.

"Alex stay here, I'll see what is going on."

While Frank went inside, Alex found a coffee can of poison in the pickup. Were they too late?

Frank was back, "Did he eat any of the tobacco worm poison?"

"No, he was just putting on, all he wanted was for the doctor to feel sorry for him. All this for one more shot."

"Don't tell mama about it, she will just nag,

then there will be another fight."

He was right, mama seemed to enjoy nagging daddy. The least said, the better.

Something was wrong, Alex knew it, the moment he jumped off the school bus. His parents were at the doorsteps waiting to tell them the bad news. His mother was crying, her hands shaking.

"Mrs. Beth's husband had an accident. He was clearing stumps, blew... himself up with a stick of dynamite. We are going over there tonight and see her and the kids. I think it would be best if y'all stayed here."

A few days after their friend's funeral, Sandra told the family that she had seen a vision from God. She convinced Robert if they did not repent of all their sins, something terrible was going to happen.

Alex had witnessed the powers of God being called down before. It was a convenient way for his mother, to get what she wanted. She became obsessed with reading the bible. Everything good was closed with "Thank you, Jesus."

One step, two-step, three-step, four, thank you, Jesus. It was enough to make Alex stop counting.

Sandra never asked Robert to go back to church, but she dragged the rest of them there. She even volunteered to help clean the sanctuary.

It was on a Sunday night, one of the few services his daddy ever attended. The preacher and some elders had selected a young man to receive the Holy Spirit. Harry was his name, and since he worked in a bank, he was a prime candidate. Harry looked a little too simple, too eager to please.

Alex and his daddy kept their eyes open during prayer, no matter the elbow nudge from Sandra. Church members clapped and sang in a fever pitch. A group of elders surrounded the young man, kneeling in front of the church.

The preacher gave praises to God and preceded to pray that God would send the Holy Spirit into Harry. The elders also prayed. All at the same time. They laid hands on him, as the preacher shouted.

"Do you feel the spirit?"

"No, not yet."

"Brother, you got to believe, God is in control. Do you have his Spirit?"

"Not yet."

Alex had never heard such an honest reply. He had misjudged Harry. By the look of it, the preacher, and the elders were getting nervous.

"Brothers and sisters, I want you to bow your heads and close your eyes and pray that Satan will no longer have a hold on him."

One elder stood on one side and one on the other. They waited for just the right moment.

"Brother, do you feel Him?" The preacher asked one more time, "Can you feel him, now?"

"Yes, yes, I feel Him, I feel Him."

"Praise God, He has washed you in the Spirit."

After they got back home, Sandra asked Robert what he thought of the service.

"I liked the part, the one where all the people stood up and acted like they were being robbed."

"Robert, why do you make so much fun of us?

"It just seems fake, you didn't see the elders punching the boy in the ribs."

"By the way, does the preacher always look at you like that? You know, like he wished he wasn't a preacher."

"Rev. Tally has enough to worry about, for people like you to be spreading rumors."

"Who said anything about rumors? Do you know something I don't? How could you like a man like that, one that lives off what people give him, he is no better than a dressed up beggar? What kind of man stays home and lets his wife work in the school lunchroom. At least I make a living for my family."

"He works part-time in Jordan's dry goods store."

"Only because Mr. Jordan is an elder in the church."

"I'm going to bed."

Daddy grabbed her arm, "You are not fooling

me one bit with all of this, thank you Jesus stuff. I will be watching you. I better never catch you with anyone else, much less that, I smell better than you, preacher."

Rev. Tally was a tall, good-looking in a suit. Alex didn't like him that much, even if he did clean up nice. Like the men in his mother's stories, most of them swept like a new broom, with no sign of wear. He could see why his daddy could be jealous of him, a man so unlike himself, a man of no work, not having to sweat and dig into the dirt to make a living for his family.

TED VICK

CHAPTER 12

*I*n spite of the spat his parents had over the church, Alex thought everything would be all right. He was wrong. A storm was coming, Frank saw to that, the day he got mad at Alex.

"Why do you think daddy, is like he is? It is because of mama. She is not right, not in her head. She didn't want you when you were born, she wanted a girl. I was only five, but I remember what happened. Mama stayed in bed weeks at the time, saying nothing, doing nothing. Daddy had to do all the cooking and cleaning and putting up a front to the neighbors.

"The doctor told daddy she might be better off in a hospital. Don't give me this, that mama is so sweet, and she loves you more than the rest of us, she doesn't. I know what she is capable of doing."

Norman was there, standing to one side, not saying anything until he blurted out.

"Leave him alone. Why are you so mean to him?"

"I forgot, you are her real favorite, why do you think that is?"

Before Norman could answer, Robert came into the room.

"Stop all the yelling, your mother might hear you?"

Why didn't daddy say Frank was wrong? Did he want to hurt me too?

A few days passed, Alex was on the porch, thinking about what had happened. His daddy came in from the field early.

"Alex, don't pay any attention to what Frank said to you about your mother. He was too young to remember all the things that happened, he got some of it wrong."

"About mama not loving me?"

"Your mother was having a hard time. You know she loves you?"

"Like I said, Frank got some stuff wrong. Just forget about it."

Robert went to the back porch to get cleaned up before Sandra came home. Alex walked out to the shed to practice, his hobby of late, throwing knives at the crib door.

"Norman, I wish we could put Frank on a wheel, you could spin him around while I try not to hit him with my knives."

"It would be better if we put a blindfold on

you, that way, you won't get into trouble if you do hit him."

They laughed, Alex was glad Norman was on his side for a change.

Frank was always running errands for Robert. Alex didn't know if it was because he wanted to do his daddy a favor. But, he did know how much Frank enjoyed driving the pickup.

Frank had been gone for a while. He went to get his daddy a pack of Camels. When he returned he seemed upset. Was it because he left with not enough money or was it something else?

"Don't worry about it. Your mama will be home soon, I guess I have enough to make it till morning."

When Sandra arrived, she made herself busy putting supper on the table, too busy to see that something was wrong with Frank. During the meal she found out what the problem was, so did everyone else.

"Robert, you look tired?"

"I cut the grass along the hedgerows today. How did the church cleaning go?"

"Except for the chewing gum stuck to the pews, it went just fine. Would you pass me a biscuit?"

His daddy managed a smile as he handed her the plate.

"You want one, Alex?"

"Yes," ma'am.

Alex broke it apart and began sopping up the cane syrup on his plate. He had not looked at Frank square on, but he could sense the tension in the air. Frank was not his usual too loud self. He was too quiet, staring at his plate, picking at the food.

"Frank, you are not eating much tonight? I hope you are not getting sick," Sandra said.

His face was red, now, and his eyes began to tear. "How can you do that? Acting like everything is all right, I'm not the one that's sick."

"What's going on, don't talk to your mother like that."

"I saw what you did, you and the preacher."

"I don't know what you are talking about."

"Frank, sit back down, you got some explaining to do. What did your mama do?"

"I stopped by the church to get some money from mama. She was not in the sanctuary. I figured she was cleaning the prayer room. In the hall I saw them, hugging."

"Oh, that. I was just hugging him bye. The pastor hugs everybody."

"It wasn't that kind of hug. I know what I saw."

"You're wrong for saying that."

"Your mother is right, it seems that part of his job is to hug up all the women."

"She was having too good of a time."

"God knows, someone around here needs to have some fun, eat your supper, your mama and I will talk about it later."

Before the night was over, Alex knew he would hear them, demons with loud and angry voices.

"I told you to stay away from him."

"It was nothing, Frank saw nothing."

"The children, they don't need a mother like you."

"And you, are you any better than me?"

"At least, people don't talk about me, not the way they do you," Robert said.

"They would if they only knew?"

"Why not leave, if that is what you want?"

"You know I have no place to go, I would if I could."

The fight, the anger, and distrust of one another killed all the hope that Alex had of his parents falling in love again. That night his mother slept with Amy.

His parents had calmed down by morning. They seemed tired, acting as if they had stayed up late playing a game. Perhaps, they liked fighting, the excitement, and drama of it all. Mama had bruises on her face. Daddy should not have hit her. How could they say such horrible things to each other and the next morning act if nothing had happened?

Could it be that the game started this morning?

It seemed longer than what it was, the few days leading up to Sunday, nothing had been said about the church. The morning came with only Alex and his mother getting ready. They plotted it together, not going with us. As they left, Alex glanced at his mother's face. Good, the makeup covered the bruise.

The absence of family members was not without notice as they walked into the church. One of the chief gossips headed their way.

"Sandra, so good to see you. I hope Robert and the rest of the family are not sick? Are they?"

"Thank you, I'm doing just fine."

With a glance toward her friends and a shrug of the shoulder, she returned to her seat.

"Mama, I'm glad you snubbed her."

"Hush, that's not nice." You should be sitting in the back with the young people."

"Not me, I hope the sermon is a short one. I know? Not a chance."

The message was about David. When Alex was younger, his mother read stories about him. Alex and David had something in common. They both liked slingshots and girls. It was an exciting story, Bathsheba on the rooftop, enjoying a bath in the washtub. I wish I could have been there.

The preacher seemed to enjoy talking about

wayward women. The kind that made themselves up with lipstick and rouge. He said they wait in the dark, like a spider, ready to devour those who pass by. To the Church of God, it was a fitting topic, seeing that most of the women believed in ugly. They were quick to say amen whenever a pretty woman was put down.

There was something not right in the church, nothing visible, not anything Alex could count. But he had endured two sermons in a row about sinning women. Someone must have seen the preacher with his mother. If something was wrong, Sandra did not look worried.

Sandra, was to busy folding the last piece of ironing, to notice the car pulling into yard. She seemed surprised when she heard the knock at the front door.

"Preacher, what brings you out this way?"

"We just wanted to make sure you are well."

"That is so kind of you, but I haven't been sick," Sandra said, looking straight at the preacher, ignoring the two men that were with him.

"Can we come in?"

"Please do but I am a little confused. You've never brought the Elders with you before."

"Sister, Morgan, the Bible states that I am to bring two witnesses when we find trouble in the church."

"Why not call me Sandra, that is what you have always called me?"

"Well… Sandra, I am just saying, certain things have caught our attention?"

"Have I done anything wrong?"

"In a way, it is just that… it doesn't seem right, the rest of the congregation sees no need in using much makeup."

"They would be better off if they did.?" Sandra said.

"We are talking about you and your soul."

"My soul, come on now, preacher, is that what you have been concerned about?"

The two men looked uneasy and began to shift their weight.

Sandra thought it best for Alex to leave the room.

"How dare you come into my home and say I am the trouble with the church?"

One of the men spoke up. "We are not saying you are the trouble, we all know Satan has that job. To put it another way, we are trying to keep you out of trouble. We are just concerned about you, that's all."

"You must be, you stare at me enough."

"This is more than makeup. Jim, why didn't you talk to me? Are you sure this was not your wife's idea?"

"Sandra, that's unfair, we want to settle this in a Christian manner. We don't want to see you leave the church."

"Your wife would like that. If looks could kill, I would have been dead a long time ago."

"Please come to the church on Sunday and repent. I will be there to pray with you."

"I will repent after you. Now, get out of my house."

Sandra was crying when Alex came out of his room.

"What are they going to do to you?"

"Nothing, darling, there is nothing they can do."

"Did they throw us out?"

"No, not you baby, I wouldn't let them do that. Maybe it would be better if we kept this to ourselves, just until I figure out what to do."

Robert and Amy returned from the store, Robert looked puzzled.

"Has Tally been here, I thought I met him down the road."

"No, I didn't see a preacher, Alex, did you?"

"No, ma'am, I was in the bedroom."

Later, she told Alex not to worry about it. "You

didn't lie to your daddy. You were talking to me, and besides, you were in the bedroom."

Alex figured his mother was just trying to put a good face on the lie. She was good at that.

Sandra was still upset when Sunday morning came around, too upset to go to the church service. That night she made up for lost time. She was determined to get things settled and if that meant bringing stuff out into the open, so be it.

His mother wore a white dress with black high heels, and her lipstick was red, very red. They sat in the same place, at the end next to the aisle. Alex saw his mama's hand grip the armrest, her fingernails digging into the stained pew, a dark stain that had softened with age. Her face stern and without a smile. Alex felt uneasy.

The preacher's wife gawked at them for a moment before heading to the back of the church. A few minutes later, she returned with her husband. With a fake smile, the preacher greeted Sandra with a noticeable lack of enthusiasm.

"Nice to see you, Sandra. I trust that you have made a decision to repent?" Sandra appeared nervous, her eyes looking into his, "It is a good day to repent. What do you think, preacher?"

"Is that a yes? I hope that is what you meant?"

"By the way, on your way to the pulpit, please tell your wife, I said hello."

Singing of old-time hymns and the sound of thunder. Mama was right, this indeed was a good time for repenting. By the time the preacher stepped behind the pulpit, the rain was loud upon the roof.

"Thank you, Jesus, for the rain, Amen. I was in the prayer room when God came a knocking at the door. 'Bro. Jim, I am going to take over.' I told Him, you can have it, Lord, I give it to you. Amen.

"That is what we all need to do with our lives, our money, we need to give it to the Lord. And tonight we have a unique service. In fact, tonight could be the beginning of the revival, here, at the Church of God. I feel God at work. Amen.

"I invite all those who need to repent to come down to the front. Come on now, God is waiting for you."

No one moved, however, the preacher did not let up. He kept looking at Sandra.

About that time, Alex's mother rose from her seat and headed toward the front. I think the preacher is in trouble. The lightning flashed, as she turned around. She looked like an angel. Alex waited for someone to say something.

"Praise God. I have talked to Sister Morgan and prayed with her. God has heard our prayers.

She comes in repentance." He looked over at Sandra, "Do you want to say amen to that, Sister Morgan?"

"I want to say more than amen? I feel the need to tell the church how very sorry I am." She hesitated for a moment, then turned her eyes toward the preacher's wife. "I am sorry, that you have closed your eyes to this woman chaser of a preacher while you spread lies and rumors about me.

"Looking nice, wearing a little makeup is that my sin? If so, Janice needs a little sin in her life. Maybe, then the preacher would want to stay home."

For a few moments, the thunder was the only sound made. Then, moans and words of disbelief spread over the congregation. To stop Sandra from saying anything else, he raised his Bible toward the ceiling and shouted, "Lord on high, I ask you in Jesus' name, that you cast the demon out of Mrs. Morgan, bring her back to us, so our church can have the victory. Brothers and sisters, can you say amen to that?"

The preacher's wife was the first to do so, then another amen from the opposite corner of the church, followed by others.

Without saying anything else, she returned to where Alex was standing.

"Can we leave now?" Alex said.

"Yes, darling we can leave"

Alex looked back to see a group of people surround the preacher in a show of their support. His wife went into the back prayer room, followed by a lady friend of hers.

Now everyone will know about the preacher. It was not mama's fault. The preacher, he was the sinner. I wonder what daddy will do?

TED VICK

CHAPTER 13

Sandra told Alex not to say anything about the church service. Said, she wanted to wait until the right time. Less than an hour later, the preacher beat her to it.

His car pulled into the front yard. By the time Robert got out to the porch, Rev. Tally was coming up the front steps. Alex's daddy stretched forth the palm of his hand, like an impatient school guard. "That is far enough. What do you want?"

"To ask you to keep your wife away from the church?"

"Now preacher, you know the church is where sinners belong."

"I don't like being called a woman chaser. I will see her in hell before she destroys me."

"Sure you will, in the meantime, keep your hands off of her."

"I have not touched your wife, Mr. Morgan."

"Frank said you were hugging her."

"I hug up all the women, it makes them feel

good, I don't mean anything by it. I am a man of God."

"That's what worries me, I don't like your smooth talk and fancy ways."

"And, I don't like your wife lying about me."

"You look uptight, preacher. Maybe you ought to let your wife help you out more often. Right now, I'm not in the mood to share mine. Of course, that could change."

Robert acted proud of the way he had humiliated him. Not to say, he wasn't mad.

"Sandra, what kind of trouble are you in now?"

"You should have been there, mama told the whole church off."

"Hush, Alex. I did no such a thing. The only thing I said was, how much I would appreciate if they would help me, by not spreading rumors."

"What made the preacher so mad?"

"I guess, my saying, if anyone saw the preacher and me together, that he was hugging me more than I was him. I told the truth. I had to save our marriage. You do believe me? The preacher just went a little crazy. His wife, she is the blame, the witch."

"Ramon can help you put a curse on her."

"Black folks are the only ones that believe in Hoodoo. Christian people use prayer," Sandra said.

"I believe in it?"

"Prayer?" Said his mother.

"No, ma'am. Hoodoo, it is a lot faster."

"Boy, you better watch your mouth, the Bible says we are to stay away from black magic and dead spirits."

Robert never said he believed what Sandra was saying. Alex thought it odd that his mother never once blamed the preacher.

To Amy's dismay, her parents were getting along better. She seemed jealous, now that her mother was getting some of her daddy's attention. For whatever reason, maybe it was hormones, but Amy started changing.

She looked older than she was. Alex noticed that some of the boys at school and even a few men at the store were now glancing her way. Although Alex had no use for Amy, he was concerned, considering how naïve she was, that she could get herself into a lot of trouble.

It was during that same time that Sam stopped by the Morgans. Any other time Alex would have thought nothing of it. But, that day was different, or perhaps he was letting his imagination get the best of him.

It was the way Sam looked at Amy. During the

sixties, a black man would have the devil to pay if he so much as looked at a white girl.

Later, a cross burned in front of Sam's house. Levi was right. People take care of there own. Maybe, no one will find out who did it. The cross-burning changed the way Sam looked at Alex. Sam was out to get him, but not like the day at the bridge.

It was in the afternoon, Alex and Buster were coming in for supper when they spotted Sam. They were quick to get out of his way. Sam was close now, speeding up he turned toward them. Alex jumped into the ditch, Buster hollowed.

In the truck's dust, Buster lay still and quiet, his leg cut. Buster are you all right, please God, let Buster be okay? He was still breathing. Alex took him home, his mother would know what to do.

"Mama, Sam ran over Buster. He did it on purpose."

His mama took a washcloth and cleaned his leg, a cut about an inch long.

"Mama, can we get a doctor?"

"Let's lay him on this blanket, he moved some, he might be all right by morning."

Alex got his mama to pray for Buster, then she turned out the light. They were alone now, it was the only time Buster ever slept in Alex's room. They were close together, close enough for Alex to feel the beat of Buster's heart.

He hoped he would be better by morning, but he wasn't. His back leg had bled through the white cloth. Buster was awake but unable to stand.

Frank thought it was a stupid idea, but Alex would not shut up until he agreed to go get Ramon. To Frank's surprise, Ramon was more than happy to see about Buster.

"Ester talked about you," Ramon said, "all of it good. Buster will be all right because you have the power to believe in something besides yourself.

"I made Buster a special suave. Put it on the cut every day for a week. By the way, I know you think Sam ran over him on purpose. I have known about the 'skinny man' all my life. You best leave him alone."

"I can take care of him, I am fourteen."

"Don't be so sure. You are dealing with more than Sam, he has powers you know nothing about."

When Robert questioned Sam. He told Robert that he did not remember seeing Alex or Buster.

"Mr. Morgan the only thing I can think of, I reached down to get an apple off the floorboard. I was on the other side of the road before I knew it, but I didn't feel a bump or anything. "

He said he was very sorry about Buster.

Alex confessed to Levi what he had done. He was the one who had burned the cross in Sam's front yard. Said, it was just a small cross and that he did not wait around for Sam to come out of his house.

"Don't think he saw me," Alex said.

"He must have to want to scare you like that. But, to hit your dog? It had to have been an accident. He never hurt anyone, not that I know. Besides, he has other ways to hurt you."

"Do you think the spirits are real? Sam says he has the power to see in the dark."

"My wife Naomi did, she was involved with dead spirits and such. Every few months, she went with a few of her friends down to Fargo to learn from a known root doctor. It was Sam, he lived there in a shack next to the swamp.

"I went with them once, stayed in the car. It scared me to death, I didn't know it could get so dark in the swamp. Pitch black it was, but there was no way I was going inside, not with them chanting fools, dancing to the light of a kerosene lantern. I didn't know which one would get me first, a gator, or a stray hant. I was lucky to get out of there alive.

"Thank the Lord, she realized she was getting in too deep. Against Sam's will, she left the group. He tried to get her back, came by the house a few times, he said the spirits sent him.

"I had to get her away from Savannah. However, Naomi never liked living out here on the farm, said blacks were better off up North. I came in from plowing one day, it was like she was never here.

"Years later, Sam showed up looking for her. For whatever reason, he stayed around these parts. I guess he was too afraid to go back to Fargo.

He messed around with the wrong person's wife. They took him out into the swamp and tied him to a bald cypress tree. For two nights, they left him there. It was a miracle, a gator didn't get him. The skeeters, pert near bit him to death, took him weeks to get over it."

"Did he call the spirits?" Alex said.

"I don't want to talk about it anymore. Spirits have brought me enough trouble, I don't like hants, dead or alive."

TED VICK

CHAPTER 14

*B*eing upset with Sam made it worse, his mind spinning and counting, forever counting things. Bedtime meant checking the house to make sure the doors were locked and if the stove was off, seven times each knob. Locks, only four times, each time counted with a mumbled voice

Revenge against Sam was as sure as counting to four. One root doctor against the other, if only Alex could convince Ramon to go along.

"I have nothing against Sam," Ramon said.

Alex said too quick, "Don't help."

Root doctors had the respect of the community. And, Ramon had no patience with Alex's attitude.

"My great-granddaddy was a witch doctor, I come from the best, and you say you are going to do it yourself, you might be white, but you are a fool. I will never help you again, just this one time, never again."

Ramon said roots and curses are the same.

They called it roots in the slave days, just in case the white folks overheard their talk. The masters had roots put on them all the time.

On a brown paper sack, Ramon listed all the things Alex would need.

(1) Buster's hair, a handful from his straw bed.

(2) Dried poison oak leaves.

(3) Black cloth.

(4) A foot of black thread.

(5) Black shoe polish.

(6) A few corn shucks.

(7) Seven Needles.

"I will make sure he knows someone has put a root on him and what kind. It will not kill him, just agitate him for a few weeks. He will pay me to get rid of the root. And, it will teach him to fear you, he won't bother you or your family again.

It was the first dark night out of seven. Alex plunged seven needles into the back of the corn shuck doll. Then wrapped it in black cloth, and tied it up, seven times around, with black thread.

After he dug a hole, he threw in a handful of Buster's hair. He covered the doll with dirt and sprinkled some dried poison oak leaves on top of it. For each night of the following six, he covered the top of the grave with the leaves. It's done, Sam deserves it.

It was hard for Alex to sleep. When will the

root jump on Sam, and how would it feel, itching nonstop and in a place that was so hard to scratch? Ramon said Sam needed to suffer for a few weeks.

Word was quick to spread. "Alex, do you know anything about Sam? Sallie May said someone put a curse on him. Who would be that stupid?"

"I thought you didn't believe in Hoodoo?"

"That was your mother, I never said I didn't."

"I guess Ramon knows who did it. Sallie May said Sam was about to itch to death."

Good, Sam had been deceived by his own mind. Alex smiled.

Robert was in his own world most of the time. In the top drawer of the dresser, Alex had a picture of him, when his daddy was young and not so thin. It was not all bad, his daddy was a good storyteller, and the family at times seemed normal.

Amy was a pain, it was wrong the way she talked about her mother. She was turning eleven, and showed no interest in boys, at least, not in front of Alex. She kept to herself for the most part.

They had not gone back to church since the night of the storm. The preacher spread it around that Sandra was nothing but trouble, a woman not right in her mind. Mrs. Baker became her ally. The more his mama heard, the worse it got.

Sandra's life had become just as exciting as the stories in the magazines. A preacher in sin, a woman scorned, what a good story. How will it end?.

"Robert, Easter is coming up, and we are still members of the church."

"Lord, woman. Are you thinking about going back? Why on earth would you want to do that?"

Robert was about to walk into a hornet's nest. If he only knew how much Sandra had not told him? They are going to kill us.

On Easter Sunday decked to a tee, they loaded down the car and took off to the Church of God. Alex hoped that God was still there. I should have stayed home with Frank and Norman.

Everybody and his brother showed up for the Easter service. What will the preacher do? He was at the door. Mama, I hope you know what you are doing?

His mother walked up to the steps as if nothing had happened. Rev. Tally was talking, not noticing her until he turned around, Sandra in his face.

"Good morning, preacher."

"And to you, Mrs. Morgan…, Robert."

Strangers were in their pew, so they sat toward the back, next to the door. The preacher's wife came over and whispered, "Sandra, why are you here? We have enough trouble, without you coming back."

Robert started to stand up when Sandra pressed her hand against his leg, "Don't even think about it, we are staying."

She turned her attention back to Mrs. Tally. "Janice, I hope you and your husband are getting along better?"

"We were," she said with heavy breath as she turned to walk away.

The singing was upbeat. However, the preacher stumbled on his way to the pulpit. Notes scattered across the floor. With the help of an Elder, the preacher gathered them up. With a red face, he asked the song director to lead the church in another hymn, as he sat in his chair and thumbed through his Bible.

The preacher stepped behind the pulpit. He was in control, and it showed on his face and in the way he moved about.

"Brothers and sisters, God snatched the sermon out of my hand and threw it on the floor. He said you will preach the message that I give you."

Then he went on for a good hour talking about how God plans to use him to grow the church. At the close of the service, with open arms, he asked the congregation if they loved him, if they loved the church?

He worked them up good. They were praying

and being slain in the spirit, saying amen to everything the preacher said.

On the way home, Alex heard more than he
wanted to about the preacher and his wife.

" I told you, Sandra it wasn't a good idea. Why
did we stay? We should have just got up and left."

"That old hag didn't deserve the satisfaction."

"Did you see the way the preacher greeted us?
Any colder and we could have killed a hog."

"Robert, I just wanted to see how they would
act toward us. Now I know what I have to do."

"To do? You have done enough."

Alex was troubled by his mother going back
to church on Easter. Why would she do that? There
had to be more to it than causing his wife more
agony. Alex noticed, there was a moment after his
mother said, "Good morning, preacher," that he
smiled.

If the rumors about her and the preacher were
true? The outcome of doing nothing would have
been worse than his mother blaming the preacher.
And, the preacher blaming it on a demon.

The insurance man said, "...all you have to do
is make up a good story." And, Sandra was an expert
in the imagination of weaving stories. After all, she
said she was working on her best one, ever.

In her story, she said, "They stay in love, no
one will ever come between them again."

His mother had sold two stories, the last one sold for three-hundred dollars. She was proud of being a writer. Alex told her how smart she was, he had never known anyone that had sold a story, much less one that was handwritten.

She asked Alex from time to time about Jennifer. She wanted to know if he still sat behind her.

"Her hair sparkles in the sunlight," Alex said.

"You are a romantic. One day, you will write your own stories."

Before the year was done, Alex would be in high school. In the meantime, there was the matter of an eighth-grade dance and graduation.

Dancing, Alex had never danced, much less held a girl close to him. His mother taught him the basic two-step.

Alex dressed that afternoon in brown pants and a white shirt. Unsure of himself, and a little embarrassed, he asked Frank to take him to the school. Some students were already there as they arrived in front of the school cafeteria. Cars had come and gone, students mingled about, including his cousin. They were still friends, but Alex never forgot the trouble John caused him. Only a few parents stayed behind, in their cars, none going inside.

The teacher and her husband greeted Alex as he walked into the room. It looked larger without the tables and chairs. There was one table in the corner, fixed up fancy, like. Napkins, the color of pink, matched the lemonade in the punch bowl.

As he sipped lemonade out of a tiny paper cup, he watched Jennifer mingle with other girls. All wore fancy dresses, fluffed out at the bottom. Jennifer had on a white skirt with a pink poodle near the hem. The blouse, also pink with those mother-of-pearl buttons. She knows she is driving me crazy.

There was no way Alex was going to be seen dancing out in the open in a room so bright. It has to be darker than this. He was prompt in asking the teacher if she could turn off some lights.

Nervous, more than ever, he struggled to get the courage to ask Jennifer for a dance. He took a deep breath. The girls were giggling as they watched Alex walk toward them. In the background, music, soft and slow. It was coming from Mr. Wade's record player. Alex was lucky, it was the only records Mr. Wade had. They were perfect for the two-step

Alex was close now, so was she. Before Alex could say anything, Jennifer was there, her hand in his. I'm going to step on her feet, I just know it. Alex was timid as he held her in his arms. How close do I get?

"You look nice, I like the lace on your blouse."

"I knew you would. I wore it just for you."

His hand touched the strap of her bra. He pulled her closer. With excitement, he two-stepped his way to cloud nine.

Before the dance was over, Alex and Jennifer walked around the edge of the parking lot. Her hand was soft, their fingers joined in a lover's lock. It was over before Alex was ready to go. There was no place to be alone. I wanted to kiss her, to feel her lips on mine, but in the end, there was no time.

Nothing was left of the night except dreams of her there, with skin so fair and stranded streams of golden hair.

The next day was the last day of school. A time to prepare for graduation services. The teacher wanted all of the students to dress for the event. Speeches were planned, and diplomas were made ready. Alex and his classmates rehearsed. Everything had to be just right.

It was Saturday night, Alex peered into the mirror, making a final pass with the comb.

"Thank you for taking me to town yesterday and for the clothes, I enjoyed shopping and getting out of school early.

"You look so handsome."

"I guess it is true. The clothes make the man."

"Are you ready to go? Be sure your pants are zipped."

"Yes, ma'am, I don't want my mule to get out."

"Lord, Alex, where did you hear that?

"June Bug."

It was a night of celebration. A few of the smart kids gave grown-up speeches. When the awards were presented, Alex received one for being the best dancer in the class. It wasn't like being an 'A' student or never missing a day, but it was his. He smiled as he glanced over at his mother, the only one of his family that attended.

CHAPTER 15

*D*espite the doctor's advice, Frank stayed and farmed the land. He believed one day the farm would be his. Robert had promised Frank a wooded homesite, about three acres, just past the creek. Even though he had put the farm into Sandra's name, Frank hoped for the best.

Norman was busy taking what did not belong to him, this time he got into trouble at school. Someone reported seeing Clarence and Norman breaking into the Vocational Building.

Norman's shop teacher and the deputy sheriff came out to the house. Robert and Norman met them at the door.

"Mr. Morgan, Norman's teacher, has reason to believe Norman took tools that don't belong to him."

Norman stood there, saying nothing.

"Can we look under the shed?"

"It's all right, I don't think you will find anything," Robert said.

Alex was in the background, Norman and Robert stayed on the porch awaiting the outcome. They returned with a toolbox and some tools.

"Mr. Cannon says the tools belong to the school shop."

"I can't believe you took those tools, Son."

"I didn't… well, I just borrowed them, I was going to take them back, honest."

The deputy asked Norman if anyone else helped him steal the tools.

"No, sir. Am I going to jail?"

"Hold on a minute. There has to be some way out of this anything to keep Norman out of jail."

"Mr. Morgan, the shop teacher, said he will forget about it, he has all the tools back. Also, the school does not want this kind of publicity. There is one condition: Norman is out of school. Agreed?"

"Yes, deputy, thank you, I'm sorry my boy caused you so much trouble."

Alex thought his daddy was more embarrassed than mad.

"Norman how could you do this, everything was getting better, and now this?"

Sandra drove up, only minutes after the sheriff had left.

"Norman are you in trouble again? I thought I saw the sheriff's car down the road?

"It was just some old tools I borrowed."

"Like you borrowed that motorcycle? What has got into you? Why can't you be more like Alex?"

"I would rather be the black sheep of the family than a mama's boy."

"That does it," Sandra said, "We are going back to church."

"What are you talking about?" Robert said.

"About us getting right with God. I belong to that church. Amy is going with us. You and Frank can stay here, but the rest of us are going."

Robert kept quiet, what could he say?

His mother, wanting to start back to church? It did not seem like a good idea. There was one bright spot, it could not get any worse than it was Easter.

In his mind, Alex saw the church as nothing more than an illusion, an amusement park by the side of the road. Above the front entrance, a neon sign sputtering, Thank You, Jesus, with every blinking breath. In the center, a merry-go-round. The music played and horses came alive. In slow motion, they lifted their heads toward the night sky.

Come on down, stop your crying, and put on a smile. For a dime, you can be a part of the show, the preacher said, behind the ticket box. Mama which horse are you going to ride, this time? How long will it be before the music stops? Before we go back to the way, it used to be?

The pain was still there, in the church of all places, would it ever end? Snide remarks, the looks of disgust, it was like being at home, except there was no mailbox out front with the Morgan name. It read, Church of God above the door? But where was God?

The game was always the same, people walked up and down the aisle, crying and carrying on like they had one foot in hell. The more guilt, the more praise, and amen from the congregation. They gave sin up on Sundays and made more during the week. The next service, they would give it up again, changing colors faster than Alex's pet lizard.

Alex had his doubts about the church. He began to see his mother in a different light. She was just as mixed up as the rest of them, maybe more. Thank you, Jesus, on the one hand, and belittling her husband on the other.

A few weeks later at the close of a fire and brimstone sermon, they sang:
Amazing grace! How sweet the sound,
That saved a wretch like me.
I once was lost, but now am found,
I was blind, but now I see.
The Pastor came down to the front.

"Oh wretched sinner, God is calling you to come and rededicate your life to him."

Sandra stepped out into the open and headed toward the preacher. What is she doing? We are in enough trouble? He put his arm on her shoulder, and had a private prayer, she whispered something in his ear.

Norman and Amy were sitting near the back. Alex did not turn around, but he wondered what they were thinking, and more so, what Amy would tell daddy?

Sandra returned to the pew without the look of any sadness. Had the hand of God touched her, or, did she walk the aisle for some other reason?

"It was a nice service, his mother said on the way home."

"What did you say to the preacher?" Amy asked.

"Don't use that tone of voice to me. It is just like you to try to make something out of nothing."

As soon as the car stopped, Amy ran straight to her daddy.

"It does not seem right Robert, you and Amy siding against me," Sandra said, as she placed her church bible on the bedroom dresser.

"Don't listen to her, daddy. You know Frank was right about her."

With a sigh, Sandra turned around to stare

Amy straight on. "And you think your daddy is so pure?

"Tell her Robert, about you and Ann Hudson."

"There is nothing to tell."

"Her husband did not think so. It seems your daddy was getting more than sweet corn from the Hudson Fruit Stand."

"You are just saying that to hurt daddy."

"It is all right, Amy, your mother, knows I like fruit stands. I stopped by a few times, just to see how things were going."

"In the barn? Her husband said he saw you and her coming out of the barn."

"I just went out there to look at the baby kittens, that is all, I swear."

"Kittens is that what you call them?"

"You know her husband is not right in the head."

"He was sober when he told me about it."

"Mama is always causing trouble like I said, don't listen to her."

"Why hate me so much, Amy?"

"The way you treat daddy, it is not right."

"That's enough, Amy. You can go to bed now."

Alex was in the hall, listening. Mama had to be making it up. It was sick, his daddy and a woman, in a barn. It was a nice thought to ponder, in the barn, on the hay, with Mrs. Hudson, Alex could picture it. She looked a lot like the girl in the magazine, under his mattress.

She was Mr. Hudson's second wife, half his age. Mama said she was a gold digger. Might be, but she was a good looking gold digger,

Alex saw it in her face, his mother had made up her mind.

"Alex, we have been through this, time and time again. You know I can't keep on living like this. There's no way I can make you understand. I don't understand it myself."

"There has to be, something more than this farm..."

"More than us?" Alex said.

"No, I didn't mean it that way."

"When you get older, you will know about passion, how it takes over, causes you to do things."

"You are right, I don't understand."

"There will be gossip, I know that, but please don't think wrong about your mother, promise me you won't do that?

"I promise."

For the next few days, Alex's mother was there, but in her mind, Sandra had already left. There was a sadness that Alex had never seen, it was there in every room, in each conversation.

It was Saturday night. Alex's mother had left early that morning and was just now returning. The moment she opened the screen door, they all knew it was time, the wait was over.

Robert was in the living room. Sandra did not say a word to him when she walked past and made her way to Amy's room. He followed and watched her gather all of her clothes.

"You know it's not right for you to leave the kids. Amy's is thirteen, she needs a woman around."

"No, Robert, all she needs is you, both of you have made that plain."

"I thought, maybe, just maybe, you would ask me to stay, to tell me you love me. That's not going to happen, is it?"

Alex pleaded for her not to leave him, he was the only one that did so.

"I'm sorry baby, I wish I could stay."

"Where are you going to live?"

"Don't know, I have a lot of things to work out."

She drove into the dark, Alex did not know if she waved back. He hated seeing her go, but the dread of her leaving one day was over.

Amy stood silent in the shadows, not even a gesture of sadness.

"You and daddy ran mama off."

"Alex, you got to be stupid, she left you too."

"Not because she wanted to," Alex said.

"You saw how she hurt daddy, you know she is crazy," Amy said.

"Never say she is crazy, you fat little pig."

"Better watch what you say, mama is not here to protect you."

The next morning the silence was broken only by the squawk of a crow. Alex was not a morning person, yet he was awake, walking around in the yard with no purpose.

No one had said anything about going to church. His daddy was on the porch, sitting, almost slumping into one of the chairs, head in his hands. Alex sensed it was more than a headache, he walked near.

"Daddy, are you all right?"

His hands, with veins, hid in plain sight, gripped the metal arms. He sat up right now.

"Sure, son. I'm just fine."

But daddy wasn't okay, not in his voice, or actions. He was the one that never cried, but I saw it, tears in his eyes.

He dropped his cigarette.

"I'll get it," Alex said.

"Alex, did she tell you where she was going?"

"I wish she had," Alex said.

Robert reached to take the cigarette back, "She

left, walked away, how could she, just walk away?"

"You could have asked her to stay?"

Robert looked away in the silence of the moment, leaving Alex to his thoughts.

Why did she leave me here, in this empty place? Empty of you, and the things you did, not the cleaning and cooking, but the things you did not say, and yet you did, with a smile, and a touch. I miss you, and this is only the first day.

CHAPTER 16

*O*ther than going to the doctor on Monday, Robert stayed around the house for the next few days. Alex knew people were talking. However, he thought no one would come right out and ask why his mother had left. He was wrong.

"They wanted to know about mama."

"What do you mean? Who asked you?"

"Mr. Higgins. At the store."

"Don't talk to him anymore. When I bought this farm, he said I moved his land stake."

Robert was not telling Alex something he did not know, he had heard it often. His daddy would never let it go, he did not like being called a thief.

"You know, he wanted the farm for himself, said I bought it out from under him."

"I know, you said you put him on your black-list."

"What did you tell him?"

"About what?"

"Your mother?"

"I didn't say anything."

"Granddaddy, what do you think he will say?"

"Say? Four words: I told you so.

"Four is my lucky number.".

"That figures?" Robert said.

Before the week ended, Mrs. Hudson came a knocking.

"Robert, I heard about Sandra. I'm so sorry."

"Thank you, there is something I want to ask you. I'll walk you to your car."

What could they be talking about? It ticked Alex off, the way she acted, as if, his mother had died. Mama was right about her.

Their family became the talk of the community. The worst part, it was all about Amy and how awful it was, a mother leaving her children. And, poor Robert, how was he going to raise her with no help?

Sinner and saint, they all wanted to know why Sandra had left. All went away empty-handed. Robert would not tell his family, much less anyone else.

Alex heard a knock and the rattle of the screen door. Could it be just another do-gooder? Sleepy from his afternoon nap, his daddy was slow to answer.

"Oh, Mrs. Walker," Robert said. Holding the door open, but not full and inviting. He joined her on the porch, Mrs. Walker, expecting Robert to welcome her in the house, stepped aside, with an uneasy look on her face.

"Did I come at a bad time?"

"Of course not. How is Ned doing?"

"You know Ned, always working."

"Amy, how is she?"

"Oh, she is doing just fine," Robert said as if nothing had happened.

"Is she home?

"Sure," looking back into the house, "Amy, come on out here."

"Amy, so nice to see you, I don't know if you remember me?"

Amy looked puzzled.

"I'm Mrs. Walker, I stopped by to see if you would like to come to my Sunday School class, all girls. I am sure you know some of them. I thought you might like getting out of the house, with your mother leaving and all."

"I go to the Church of God."

Robert looked over at Amy. You have not gone there for a while, I think you can fit into the Baptist Church."

"Whatever, I'll go if you want me to. Who will take me?"

"Why you can go with me, I come right by here on my way to the church," Mrs. Walker said.

"I will pick you up next Sunday. I know you

will enjoy it." Mrs. Walker seemed thrilled.

The moment Robert and Amy came back into the living room, Amy showed her wrong side.

"Why do you want me to go, you know they will laugh at me? No, I'm not going."

She pouted until supper, such as it was. Since Sandra left, the meals had more to do with not starving than something Alex enjoyed. Where was the fried chicken and banana pudding?

"Amy, it would look better if the community saw you going to church."

Back to Amy, it is always, Amy.

Robert made sure Amy went to church with Mrs. Walker. However, to think Amy's going to church would somehow help their situation did not happen, it only made it worse. Not that Amy did not like going, it was just the opposite. She became friends with Mrs. Walker, perhaps too good of friends.

Alex saw a car pull up. It was Mrs. Walker and another lady. The moment they got out of the car, Alex could sense a tightness in the air.

"Hi Alex, is your sister and daddy home?"

"I'll go get them," Alex said, knowing better than to invite them inside.

"What could they want?" His daddy mumbled

as he walked to the door, Amy following along.

"Hello, Amy," Mrs. Walker said. "Robert, we have some news, I think you will like it"

The two women insisted on going inside. Robert hesitated, then gave in.

"Y'all can sit over on the couch," Robert said, looking at the stranger with Mrs. Walker.

"Robert, this is Mrs. Phillips, we wanted to talk to you about something that might help Amy."

"I didn't think Amy needed any help."

"Well, you might not think so, and that is understandable, but we are looking at it from a female's point of view. Amy is here with nothing but boys, that might develop into a problem."

"I can handle my boys. We are not heathens, you know."

"I am sure you can, but Amy needs an environment that would suit her needs as a young lady."

"You can't take her away from me. Is that what you are talking about?"

"No," Mrs. Phillip interrupted, "I manage a place for girls like Amy."

"Like Amy?"

"I'm sorry, I did not mean it in a bad way. There are quite a few girls who have been abandoned by their mothers. It would be a nice place for Amy. She will get education, as well as room and board. It would be a great opportunity."

"If it doesn't work out, can Amy come back home?"

"Of course," Mrs. Phillips said, "There is no hurry. We will come back next Saturday, you can tell us your decision then."

As they left, Robert looked at Amy, "Who have you been talking to, the preacher? What did you tell Mrs. Walker about us?"

"Nothing, daddy."

"You said something, for them to be out here. Did you see the way they were looking at the place?"

"You are not going to send me to that girl's school, are you?"

"I don't have a choice, not now. If you don't go, you know what will happen? The state, they will force you to go, and there might be no way to get you back.

"Just try it out a few days, if you get homesick, start crying. They will have to bring you home."

Robert was paranoid about the government, he saw nothing in it for Amy. One thing was for sure, Robert was not willing to be without Amy for very long.

Alex asked Mr. Wade, what was the law concerning Amy, now that his mother had left her. He assured Alex there was no reason for the State to take Amy away from her home. The ladies were only trying to help. It eased Alex's mind.

It worked out for Robert, Amy was back home. Why did Mrs. Walker want Amy out of the house? Daddy was right, Amy said something that aroused suspicion.

Amy seemed happy to be on Roberts good side again. She would do anything for her daddy. When he mentioned her weight, she took off a few pounds.

Alex told her it was nothing she did. It was the meals they had to eat, no dessert, not the first one since their mother left.

How could daddy act like nothing is wrong when mama's chair was empty of her smile and table talk?

Norman asked Frank for another biscuit.

"Here, have some syrup to go with it."

"Biscuits and syrup that's all we seem to have any more," Norman complained.

Alex said, "That's not true, we have black-eyed peas, I hate black-eyed peas. Daddy, when is mama coming home?"

"She's never coming back," Amy said.

"I was talking to daddy."

"Alex, eat your peas and don't say any more about the peas or your mother."

There were things he wanted to say to his daddy, but he figured there was no use.

The house was quiet now, and the smell of a woman's perfume was missing from the kitchen. Everyone was in bed, except Alex. He sat down at the table next to his mother's chair.

The stories she wrote were more about her than other people. She was Sandra by a different name. Perhaps she wanted to be that farm girl in the trashy magazine? But, she wasn't the girl of her imagination, the one that found love. She was Robert's wife, and she was my mother, with three other kids, no amount of writing could change that.

The farm was in good hands with Frank, he was twenty now, and seemed content. Robert gave him a large share of the crops and let him make most of the decisions. Willie was helping more now. The farm was turning a profit.

Out-of-place things happened after Alex's mother left. Norman closed in the shed and added on to the back. He and Clarence worked together buying and painting cars. They sold them out of town. Norman had learned his lesson with little Jimmy Baker.

They offered Alex a job sanding down the cars for paint. Alex refused. He wanted no part of it. The least he knew the better off he would be. His daddy said no more about Clarence being from white trash, Alex wondered why? Mama would put a stop to it.

No matter how crazy his mother was, she was the one that held the family together. She was the spiritual one. To Alex, she did not enjoy sinning, his daddy forced her into it.

Robert never mentioned missing Sandra. However, Alex felt sorry for him, the way he walked around, empty, with only a few words to say. He laughed as much as a sad face could.

Sandra left four months ago. Granddaddy said she must have gone back to her folks in Columbus, Georgia. He called them nothing but a bunch of snuff dippers. Alex could see why his mother did not get along with him.

It was Saturday morning, Robert had gone into town to check the corn prices. He was back much sooner than Alex thought. His daddy was fast pulling into the yard and slow to get out.

Alex knew something was wrong when he slammed the door, hard enough to make the window rattle. Robert walked toward the house, mumbling. Alex, could not understand a word until he came closer and louder.

"You won't believe it, you just won't believe it, your sweet little innocent mama. Guess who she ran off with?"

His voice trembled beneath a face of anger.

"Tom Atkins. She went to the Five and Dime, all right, but it wasn't, just to buy those dirty magazines. It must have been going on for a long time. Those birds, he gave them to her, my ass."

Alex felt sorry for his daddy. However, his mind spun around, your ass daddy? It wasn't your ass. Bad Alex. He focused, once more on Robert.

"I'm sorry, I swear, I didn't know, I thought it might be the preacher, she was telling the truth all along."

"I knew you would make the whore out to be a saint."

"Don't call her that she is not a whore. It is your fault, I saw her, that night, begging you to say it, to say you loved her. You left her there, on the floor, crying. It is your fault, mama is gone."

"Why you..."

Alex put his hand up, but not in time to stop the slap to his face.

"I'm not mama," Alex mumbled through thick lips.

There was nothing else said. As usual, Alex walked away. It was the better thing to do. The Bible says we should honor our parents, I guess that means both of them.

Chapter 17

There was never a for sale sign out in front of the Five and Dime. Without a word, Mr. Atkins walked away one day, and the new owner was there the next. He left his wife the house, car, and most of the money.

If not the entire town, at least the members of the Baptist church could not believe Mr. Atkins would leave his wife. He was a man who prayed in public and gave more than his share of money to his church.

To Alex, it was strange. The church-going people, the ones that said they believed in God, were the first to run away from Him, to do bad things, like his mother. However, his daddy would never have walked out on his family.

Robert referred to Mr. Atkins as the 'ten-cent man.' But, no matter how much he downgraded him, he was with Sandra, and there was nothing he could do about it.

Alex hoped his mother would find happiness, but how could she, leaving behind her family and taking away another man from his wife. As young as Alex was, he knew, God would never bless them, not until they repented of their sin. Alex prayed that he would never be like her,.Although, his love for her remained.

Alex went back to Levi's, he felt secure there. He drove the pickup, he could do so, as long as he stayed on the dirt road. As soon as he opened the door, Boo came to meet him. Levi was sitting on the steps. Two fishing poles lay on the edge of the porch.

"Hello, Boo, I missed you, girl."

"I will be there in a minute, I got to see how Molly is doing."

Alex spent a few minutes stroking her mane before heading over to the steps.

"It has been a while, Mr. Morgan."

"You always say that."

"No harm in telling the truth."

"I made you a pole, got the worms too."

"How did you know I was coming?"

"I didn't. I have had the poles for a week, hoping you will come by. The worms I keep in the can, anyway."

They made their way through the fields, already harvested and waiting for spring.

"God has a plan for everyone, even your mother. Don't worry, God is watching over your mama."

"I pray every night, just like she said. I pray for you and Boo."

"Thank you, Alex. You know...We love you."

"You do, you really do? I love y'all too."

It was an awkward moment. Nothing else was said until they reached the fishing hole.

"Reckon there are any alligators around here? Frank said there is one under the bridge."

"Your brother is just trying to scare you."

"I thought so. Look, you got something on your line?"

"See Alex, you bring people good luck."

Between them, they caught enough for a mess.

"Here, you can have mine, I just came by to talk to you and Boo."

"Well, it looks like Boo is ready to go back. It was nice being with you, Mr. Morgan."

"I am the one that needs to call you Mr."

Levi laughed as he put his hand on Alex's shoulder.

"Now, what do you think your daddy would say to that?"

"What would he say?" Alex smiled.

Walking in the field with Levi, made Alex believe he was nine again, long before he knew about adult things.

By Christmas, it was as if his mother had died. If so, she was resurrected at 8 o'clock in January 1962. Lights from a stranger's truck flashed against the living room wall. A short, plump man stepped out into the headlights, the motor still running. Norman recognized him.

"Daddy, you are not going to like this?"

Robert stepped out to the porch, it was Mr. Higgins.

"I guess I'm the last person you expected to see?"

Robert stood still, not answering,

"I see you have kept good care of the place.".

"Get to the point, what are you up to?"

"I met with your wife today."

"Sandra? What does she have to do with this?"

"She called me, said she had something I wanted."

"My farm?" Robert said.

"It was her farm, you signed it over to her when you went into the hospital, remember? It is all legal, my lawyers made sure of that, here is your copy of the paperwork."

"What kind of person are you? To buy a man's farm out from under him. You know you are wrong for that?" Robert said.

"I am sorry it has to be this way. Here is your

check. It isn't much. She said you can keep the house and three acres."

"How much did she sell it to you for?"

Mr. Higgins looked toward the ground, his voice low. "Sixteen Thousand," he said.

Robert stepped closer, "Two-hundred dollars an acre, you didn't buy the place, you outright stole it."

"I am sorry you feel that way."

Mr. Higgins turned around to leave and turned back again. "I almost forgot, I guess you won't need the farm equipment. I will give you a fair price."

"That will be a cold day in hell."

As soon as Mr. Higgins left, Robert took the shotgun and headed for the truck. "She is not getting away with it."

"Put the gun back, daddy," Frank pleaded. "No need for you to go to jail, what would Amy do,?"

"I have to go, maybe I'll just talk to her."

It was almost twelve when he returned. "She skipped town." Empty of anything else to say, he sat on the couch and stared, into the unknown, into his thoughts.

Amy stayed with him for a while. There was nothing anyone could do, except wait.

It was a heavy load for him to bear, his wife, and now his land gone? Alex prayed for his daddy. Not mama, I will not pray for her, not tonight.

The next morning Robert said it was not some spur-of-the-moment thing, what Sandra had done. "She planned it all along, why else would she have taken the deed? The conniving witch.

"There must be a reason she did not sign the house over to me. She wants me to worry. If she ever sells it, I swear on the Bible, I will kill her."

Alex did not understand evil and how it crawls inside a person, to change and destroy all the happiness it finds. It was a sorry thing for a mother to do, to leave her children, to sell their land. I promised her I would not think ill of her, but I don't know if I like her anymore.

Robert told Frank to sell the tractor and other equipment. All of Frank's hard work, for nothing. The land that his daddy gave him, in the pines, beyond the creek, will never be his.

"Just like that, you are giving up?"Frank said.

"There is nothing we can do. I never thought your mama would run off with another man, much less, sell the farm."

"You should have never, put it in her name. If it is all right with you? I'll stay here as long as I can. There has to be a way we can make a living?"

"If I didn't have these headaches, I wouldn't need any shots. I might try the operation that Dr. Johnson suggested."

"Boring holes in the side of your head? Is that

what you want? He also said you could die. Besides, that was when you first had the headaches, it won't do any good now?

"What do you mean by that? You know I take the shots because I hurt."

"I know, daddy. Just the same, it is a crazy idea. We will make it, you know we will make it?"

The month of March came and went, and so did Alex's Sixteenth birthday. There was no cause for celebration.

His daddy's eyes were dull, and his steps slow, no reason to do so, except there was no place to go. Robert spent his days in the chair on the porch, watching strangers work the land.

As long as Frank and Norman got into town on Saturdays, they seemed content. Alex was old enough to drive, a good thing considering the amount of beer his brothers drank.

One night they got a hold of something different.

"I told you he sold shine." Frank took a sip out of the quart jar and wiped his mouth.

"Wow, it's got a kick to it."

He passed it to Norman, "You gotta try some if you think you are man enough?"

Norman seemed reluctant at first. Not wanting to look like a wimp, he pressed the jar to his lips. It was just enough to call it a sip, but it made Norman look more grown-up.

"I can't believe they can sell this stuff. It tastes awful."

"The black juke joints buy it all the time. There is a big demand for it in Albany."

Frank ended up in the ditch, wallowing in the mud. He wasn't so happy later when he vomited up a foul-smelling foam. The next day, the shine business was all Frank talked about.

"I have been thinking about this for a while. I know a black man who makes the stuff. He's a sharecropper."

"What does that have to do with anything. Besides Clarence and I make a little cash."

"Like the motorcycle? I thought for sure they were going to put you in jail."

"I'm careful. Besides, we do repairs. Mrs. Mason is bringing her car by tomorrow."

"That white Plymouth? What are you going to do to it?"

"Plugs and points, maybe set the timing."

"How much is it going to cost? Norman said.

"Cost?"

"Yeah, Frank, how much do we need, you know, you did mention going into business."

"Maybe nothing. Can you get Mrs. Mason to leave the car with you a few days?"

"I must be missing something? What are you talking about?"

"It is my best idea, ever. If we put a fake antenna on it, you know, the kind that flops over, it will look just like a cop car. Mrs. Mason will never know."

"I don't even want to hear it," Norman said.

"Hold on Norman, I can't do this without you. It will be clear profit. You can drive by his house if he has the shine close by it will scare him into moving it."

"Let me play the GBI man. I'm old enough to drive," Alex said.

"I don't know it might be too dangerous."

"I'm brave?" Alex said.

"See, Norman even your kid brother is willing to help me. We can do this, no one is going to get hurt, I promise."

The following night, they arrived at the lane that ran past the black man's house.

"Put the shades on, do it just like I said."

"I know, drive slow and don't stop."

"And remember, there is no place to turn around. You got to drive by the house to the other road."

Alex started the motor.

"Good luck, Norman said, "We will see you later."

This might not be a good idea. I told them I would do it, I guess I will.

Alex started down the lane. He was close now, a light glowed inside the house. People were on the porch, he could not see how many. What if they try to stop me? If they do, I have no way out.

Alex made it to the end of the lane. Turning onto the highway, he saw lights behind him. He stepped on the gas. Someone yelled.

It was Frank, poking his head out of the window of the pickup.

"Why didn't you stop? Couldn't you see us?"

"I thought they were after me, I cannot see out of these glasses."

"Well, at least it worked. The shine was in the tobacco barn. As soon as you drove past the house, he moved it to the cotton patch. We are going back to get it. Take the pickup and wait for us at the church down the road."

Frank and Norman drove the car down by the side of the man's house.

"Close enough," Frank said, "to touch the bur headed boy, hanging out the window."

We scared them good. They just watched as we run over the cotton.

"I admit it," Norman said, "I thought we were

in trouble, for sure. We had no choice, but to go back the same way."

"Yeah, and with their shine, black people just can't figure things out," Frank said.

"Well, if they do, what if they find out it was us?"

"Do you think they would be crazy enough to go after a bunch of white boys?"

TED VICK

Chapter 18

*A*my was changing and not for the better. She was mean to everyone, even daddy. She didn't talk much at all, and for the most part, stayed in her room. Given the heat, it was unusual for her to do so. Robert said she had a summer cold. Alex knew there had to be more to it than that.

It was the second day, Amy had not come out, not even to go to the bathroom. Robert had been in and out of her room all day. Dark was falling, he seemed nervous as he started to the door.

"Stay out of Amy's room. I'm going to get the doctor." Frank and Norman went outside. If Robert said something to them, they did not tell Alex.

Perhaps there was a place inside of Alex that knew what was going on. His mother was the first one to go. Maybe, she blamed herself. She was not as bad as people said. Even his daddy was quiet about her until she ran off the 'ten-cent man'.

His daddy returned with the doctor. They were in the yard now. Alex saw the glow of his daddy's cigarette as he tossed it to the ground. Words were loud and unfriendly. After a few minutes, they walked into the living room.

"Where is she?"

Robert pointed to Amy's bedroom door

"I'll call you if I need you."

As he entered the room, Alex heard him speak to Amy, his voice soft and caring. He stayed only a few minutes.

"It is a mess. You should have called me sooner. Amy is not doing good. Get me all the clean towels you can find and a pan of hot water."

Robert made it clear, he wanted all the boys to stay out of the way.

"You should have called me," the doctor said again, shaking his head as Robert gave him the pan and towels.

Alex heard Amy moan. She is in pain. Why won't someone tell me what is wrong?

Robert stood close to the room. A half-hour passed, then silence. The doctor opened the door part way, said he needed a bucket.

"A bucket?"

"Yes, a bucket."

Robert turned to Alex, "I think there's one in the crib."

In a few minutes, Alex returned.

"My Lord, Alex. A slop bucket?"

"It was in the yard. It is dark in the crib."

"Give it to me. A guess it don't make much difference."

It was over. Dr. Johnson's voice seemed sad, "I gave Amy a shot, to help her sleep. Y'all need to let her rest."

"I want to talk to you?" He said, looking Robert straight on, his voice stern.

They walked to the doctor's car. There was a silence about their conversation until the doctor raised his voice. By the sound of it, he was upset, if not downright mad.

"Robert, I got to report it. It is the law." There was nothing else said.

That night Alex saw fear in his daddy's face. The fear of not knowing what to do, when cheeks suck in, and eyes go full. What is going on, I think daddy is in trouble?

"Is Amy going to be all right?" Frank asked.

"Just female trouble, nothing we can talk about, nothing anyone needs to know. Been a long day, I need to clean Amy's room. Boys, y'all can go to bed, there is no need to stay up any longer."

The next day Alex saw fresh dirt behind the chicken house. Daddy was right, there was nothing anyone needed to know.

Just before supper, the sheriff's car pulled into the yard, parking sideways like he owned the place.

The knock was heavy upon the screen door. Robert seemed nervous, hesitating to answer.

"What brings you out this way?"

"Mr. Morgan, I would like for you to come out to the car. I need to ask you some questions."

Alex turned to Frank, in a low voice he asked, him if he knew what kind of questions.

"Like I know? Do you think I am a mind reader?"

"They are going to lock him up," Alex said.

"Daddy hasn't done anything wrong. You like causing trouble. You're as bad as your mama."

Fifteen minutes later, the officer and Robert came back into the house.

"Are you sure you need to talk to her? She has been through enough," Robert said.

"I won't be but a minute."

Robert stood close to the door, trying to overhear. He was quick to step away when the door began to open. The officer closed his notebook.

"I know you are upset, Mr. Morgan. But, let me ask you again, are you sure she is telling the truth? Could it have been a boy a school? Someone she wants to protect?"

"There is no need for any more questions, I told you, she has never mentioned a boy to me."

"Well then, I'll go over and talk to Sam, first thing in the morning. Don't say anything, I want to get to the bottom of this before someone does something crazy."

Alex didn't sleep much that night, all he could think about was Sam. The next morning he got the courage to ask his daddy about him.

"No one said anything about Sam?"

"Don't use that tone of voice with me. It is none of your business."

"I don't understand. What is going to happen to Sam?"

"What do you care, I thought you hated him?"

"I'm telling all you boys, you better leave this be. I don't want anymore said about it."

It was Sunday, the day of sermons and forgiveness. But that Sunday was different, it was the first day Alex had ever seen Levi upset. He knew something was wrong, Levi was driving faster than usual. He turned his truck into the yard, pulling up to where Alex was standing.

"Mr. Simmons came by just before Sunday School and told us about Sam. He said he saw the Klan down at his farm last night, burning a cross and carrying on. From the sound of the dogs, he figured Sam headed for Pope's Pond.

"The preacher said it wasn't right to leave one of

our own in the woods. So, we went over there in my pickup. There wasn't a soul around, just beer cans and tire tracks. And, a trail of blood from the gallberry bushes to where they hung Sam.

"He was hanging from a white oak, twisting in the wind, one foot was gnawed off. We laid him out in the back of the truck, covered him up with an old canvas. Sam didn't deserve a death like that. It ain't right what y'all did to him. He was a little strange, but he never meant anyone harm.

The story I told you, the one about Sam. There was more to it . They not only tied him to a tree and left him in the swamp. They cut him, like a pig in a pen. No way, he was after your sister or any other girl."

"Where is he now?"

"Down at the church, don't want to bury him with all that blood on him. No white man would be done like that."

Alex hoped that Levi didn't blame him. He had never heard him say much about black and white before. Sam is already dead, best I keep quiet. Why do I have to keep their secrets? I'm tired of secrets.

Robert and his family said nothing, they only listened as others talked about the hanging. It was not mentioned in the Morgan household until Alex cornered Amy in the kitchen.

"You are lying. Sam didn't do anything to you."

"Keep quiet, daddy said we are not talking about it."

"Why did you tell the sheriff it was Sam? You know you and daddy killed him, the same as if you were there."

Amy, started crying, she ran out of the kitchen and into the yard where Robert was. He stood still for a moment before walking with Amy back to the house.

"Alex, come out here," he yelled from the front porch."

He was mad, Alex saw it on his face as he opened the screen door.

"Why are you bothering your sister?"

"Sam did not hurt Amy. I have proof."

"Are you crazy? What kind of talk is that?"

"I am not the one who is crazy. I know why mama left. I heard her that night," Alex said with tears, his lips thick against cheeks that quivered.

"You heard nothing."

"Tell him to leave daddy, we don't need him around."

Alex saw the hurt in his daddy's face and wondered why he had said anything.

Robert hesitated. "I hate to say it, but everybody might be better off if you did leave. I don't think you ever liked it here much, anyway."

Alex was slow to walk back into the house. A

place where he was no longer wanted.

He placed his clothes in a paper sack and tied it to his bicycle. It was over now, he hoped that all the secrets would be left behind, there in that six-room house, with a hall down the middle.

Before leaving, he held Buster in his lap. I wish I knew what to say to him. He could not go, not with his bad leg, and age. A part of Alex wished his daddy would say he had changed his mind. He didn't. Alex headed down the road toward the store.

"No Buster, go back. You have to stay." Alex doubled back to Levi's house. He would know what to do. It was not that Alex liked black people, but he did like Levi.

"Alex, what is going on? Why you got your stuff with you?"

"Daddy… He ran me off, said he didn't need me no more."

"You can't stay here, someone might see you."

"I don't know any place to go?"

"You got your granddaddy. He might take you in."

"He has no use for daddy, he is not the kind to take in one of his kids."

"Here, give me your clothes. You better hide your bicycle around back. You can stay for a few days, and then you got to go. I don't want to end up like Sam."

Levi was right, both of them were in danger, the more so, the longer Alex stayed.

"There's got to be somebody that will take you?"

"Mama, but I don't know where she is."

"You are in a mess. I think both of us are. What did you say to your daddy that made him so mad?"

"He would kill me if he were to find out I told you. I better not say."

"I'll figure out what to do, in the meantime, stay out of sight, no telling what your daddy would do if he finds you here."

Levi hired someone to take Alex someplace else. It was the only thing he knew to do.

"You sure y'all want to do this? We gonna have to cover him up with these blankets. I don't want to get caught hauling a white boy around."

"You take care of the boy, put him out at the church like I told you."

Alex crawled into the back.

"Behave yourself, you got my address."

Alex grabbed his hand. "Now Alex, it will be all right, the church folks will take care of you, at least until you get settled."

Levi closed the tailgate.

"He's ready now."

Alex looked back until there was no more Levi

to see. As he pulled the blanket over his head, he felt the last bump of the lane before the truck turned onto the dirt road. I forgot to tell Boo and Molly bye. It will be a long ride. I'm not afraid.

Except for blacks in the back of a truck, a black and a white did not travel together, not on the open road, not in the Deep South. Alex remained for the most part beneath the blanket. There was fear, in every sound of a passing car, and the stopping and going of the pickup.

Alex knew where he was going, but not where he was headed. He was sure of one thing, he was not wanted, not by his family. He wished he could have stayed with Levi, Buster would have liked Boo.

The pavement faded into the jar of a country road, leaving behind the sound of traffic and the lights of Savannah. Alex threw back the cover, he was free to stand, to feel the wind in his face. The sun was peeking over distant trees, its rays revealing vast fields of farmland.

Turning right at the fork, Alex saw the church in the distance. It was smaller than Alex expected but well attended by the looks of the yard in front, bare as a bone with not a sign of any grass.

The church seemed at home, tucked in be-tween two giant oak trees. It was covered with pine boards, old and brown, with no trace of paint.

The man helped Alex get his belongings out of the truck. "We moved along, faster than I thought. Someone will come by soon."

"I never did catch your name?" Alex said.

"Sam."

"I knew a Sam once," Alex said.

"Sam, the man from New Orleans? The man they lynched?"

"Yes, sir."

"It was too bad about Sam. You got to be careful nowadays. I'll be leaving you now. Levi wanted me to be sure to tell you that everything will be all right."

"Thank you for bringing me."

"No thanks to me, Levi gave me the money."

"If you see him, tell him, would you tell him for me?"

"I sure will, you take care now."

Alex sat on the top step and leaned his head against the front door.

I noise of a car, Alex woke to the sight of a well-dressed man. It was good to see someone with happy steps and a warm smile.

"You must be Alex? Of course you are. You don't find too many white boys sitting in front of a Negro church. I'm Rev. Joseph Hezekiah, most folks call me Bro. Joe."

"Yes, sir."

"You got manners. I like that. I bet you are hungry? You got to be after that long trip. Put your bike in the back of my truck. The wife is waiting for us. I was surprised to hear from my brother. The last time I saw him was when I was ordained."

The preacher lived not far from the church. His house better than most, and a dog that reminded him of Buster. On the porch in a rocker was a lady with a store-bought dress. She was quick to her feet, short in statue and without any smile at all.

"Ellie, I want you to meet Mr. Morgan."

"Just call me Alex."

"Well, Alex, you might as well come on into the house."

Mr. Howard, the chain gang boss, had a better personality. I miss Levi.

She didn't join them at the table, but that didn't stop her taking. She spoke to her husband like Alex wasn't even there.

"You must be crazy. You know the boy don't belong here, he needs to be with his own kind."

"Ellie, it's just for a few days, I promised Levi I would help him find work and a place to stay."

"You should have asked me first."

"Alex needs some rest, tomorrow I will take him to River Street. There's plenty of work. Most of the young men are over in Vietnam."

"Levi said he was my age when he worked on the docks."

"We both did, that is, until Levi joined the service. He went into the Army, and I came back to the farm. I think I made the better choice? Levi was never the same."

"Levi is my friend."

"Didn't mean anything by it, just that war changes people, some more than others."

"He better sleep in the barn. I don't want anybody talking about us," Ellie said.

What was it about the color of my skin that made her reject me? I wish I could have stayed with Levi. Frank was right, I might be a little slow, but to fear the thoughts of others, is something I will never understand.

Morning came. I am nervous but not afraid.

TED VICK

CHAPTER 19

*A*lex remained in Savannah, and through the years
he would often travel to see Levi. Sixty-seven
would prove to be a difficult year for Alex. He longed
for days gone by when he sat on the porch and talked
with his new friend.

Now, the fields around his house lay in a stillness that belongs only to the dead. Molly's plow
leaned against the side of her crib, coated in rust.
Levi lost heart after she died, said he didn't want to
train anyone else.

He talked more than ever before, about a place
beyond his view. The pain of living had taken its
toll. He wanted to be young, to feel the passion for
life, again. That wasn't going to happen if he stayed
here.

"Winter will be here before you know it," Levi
said, "I can feel it in my bones. I hope Boo goes
before me. I don't want her to be alone."

"You know I'll take care of her."

"I know you will, I remember when you came

looking for a place to fish. You were just a boy and Boo, she was only a few years old. A lot of time has passed us by, Boo is fourteen now. As you can see, she still gets around good, maybe better than me. I got her on Halloween, she was just a little puppy."

"She scared me the first time I saw her. Boo was a good watchdog," Alex said.

"Still is, she can spot a person coming a mile away. Just the other day a young boy from across the way came nosing around, she chased him clear to the road."

"Do you want me to have a talk with the boy? I don't like anyone bothering you."

"Nah, he was just a small fellow, don't think he meant any harm. I hope you can stay the night, you can put blankets on the floor?"

"I'll take you up on that. It will be a while before I can get back to see you. Are you sure you will be all right? Do you need any money?"

"You don't have to keep bringing me stuff, you act like I can't do for myself. Not that I don't appreciate it, you know I do."

Into the night, they sat by the fire, Boo on the floor between them. For once, Alex let Levi do most of the talking, about the past, the good more than the bad. Just before bed, Alex read a chapter from the Bible. Like his mother, Levi did all the praying.

His mind was never far from Levi. He is just having a rough time, he will snap out of it soon. Like he said, he is not going before Boo, and she has a few more years. Alex tried to convince himself.

It had been a long trip, he was glad to be back in a familiar place. He stopped in Thomasville for gas. It was nice to see the town again, to wave at people that waved back.

Hanging the hose back, he turned to walk into the store. Of all the luck, standing next to the front door, Mr. Higgins chewing the fat with another farmer. Alex walked past them to pay the clerk.

"Alex, I thought that was you. It's been a long time. You have grown up on me. Does your daddy know you are in town? Oh, that's right, I heard you two are not getting along. Someone said he threw you out."

"By the looks of your stomach, you've been doing some growing too," Alex said.

"There is no need to be nasty."

"Look who's talking, at least I don't have to go through a man's wife to take his land. I have a mind to teach you a lesson."

"I see you still have a mean streak in you."

"On second thought, you are not worth my going to jail. Besides, if you keep on eating you will be dead soon enough."

As soon as Alex got the upper-hand, he paid the clerk. There was nothing else said. He pulled out onto the highway, leaving Mr. Higgins alone with his stare.

That did not help you, any. I know. Why are you so angry? Leave me alone. I have to stop this, the talking to myself.

Seeing Mr. Higgins caused Alex to think of his own family. Asking Levi about them was one thing. But, to drive by the old home place, he saw no need until today. The turnoff was just ahead.

Unsure of what to do, he stopped by the side of the road. Beyond the stop sign was the field, the place where the fossil rock was found, and arrowheads on top of the ground.

The road that ran in front of the house was paved now. Did it all happen the way mama said? Is it only in my mind, in places of forbidden thought? Like dead people, my secrets haunt me. It is time to go back. I'm afraid.

Flooded with memories, he pulled into the yard in front of the barn. Norman was under the shelter, the same as on the day Alex left.

"I thought it was you. Nice car. Where you been?"

"It's a long story, how y'all doing?"

"Just getting by."

"I heard Frank got drafted?"

"No, he signed up. He will be coming home next month. Daddy will be glad to see him."

"Buster, I guess he passed away?"

"Soon, after you left, he just stopped eating. We buried him out back, under the tree you use to climb."

"Daddy still taking shots?"

"Some, not as much as before."

"Amy don't go out much, stays with daddy most of the time. They are up at the house now."

"It has been long enough, I reckon," Alex said, as he started his walk to the house.

Part of me wants to be here, to talk to daddy, and yet I don't want to. I keep telling myself, I can do this. I see him in the chair, on the porch, Amy standing behind him. They see me.

"Is that you?"

"It's him," Amy said, in a hateful tone of voice.

"How are you doing, daddy."

"Don't call me daddy, you are not my son, I don't know you anymore. No son of mine would disgrace his family's name by hanging around with black people."

"The family name was disgraced a long time ago," Alex said.

"I heard all about you and Levi. You need to thank me. I'm the reason you didn't get hurt."

"What are you talking about?"

"You spending weekends with him. A thing like that don't happen without somebody noticing.

"They came by some years back, asked me to put a stop to it. I told them I should've done that when you were a boy. I figured you would grow out of it. "

"Grow out of what? You act like respecting other people is some kind of disease?"

" Who came by?"

"Like you don't know? They said they were not going to let it go, 'the last thing we need is whites living with blacks.' Even if it was just an old black man, someone had to suffer."

"He didn't tell you, did he? About what happened, what they did, when Levi said he would never ask you to stay away."

"They hurt Levi?"

"No, but the mule did not fair as well. Levi didn't give up farming because he wanted to.

"You could have talked them out of it?"

"Why would I? They did the right thing."

"To kill Molly?"

"Molly?"

"Yes, the mule. Her name was Molly.

"What brings you back?"

"You tell me a thing like that, then ask my reason for being here, like we are having an everyday conversation."

"Damn you," I came here to tell you I forgive you, and this is what I get? Why didn't you try to stop them? Do you hate me so much? Are you that jealous of Levi?"

"Jealous?"

"Yes, of a man that loves me more than you?"

"Jealous of a black man, you must be crazy?"

"That is what you called mama."

"Stop it," Amy said, "We don't want you coming around here. Daddy can run you off again."

"Run me off? Like I want to stay"

"Maybe you are right, you are not my daddy, you haven't been since I was five."

"Amy go into the house, I need to talk to Alex alone." Robert waited until she closed the door before returning his stare to Alex.

"Frank was telling you the truth about what happened when you were born. Your mama and me were going through some rough times. She wanted a baby girl more than anything else."

"She didn't want me?"

"Alex it was not about you. That is your problem. You think everything is about you. Your mama just wanted a girl. And all I wanted was your mother to be happy. Something happened after you were born. She was never the same.

"She said the last thing she wanted was another baby. When Amy came along. It was too late. Amy was too late. Your mother never took a liking to her."

"It was different for me, Amy was my joy, still is. I would do anything to protect her. When Sam hurt her, I asked the doctor not to bring the sheriff into it. Told him, I was going to take care of it. Amy was damaged goods. Do you think anyone would want her if they knew she was raped by a black?"

"He couldn't do that...Levi said..."

"That the white boys castrated him? The sheriff checked with people in Fargo. It never happened. Sam made all of it up."

"Why didn't you tell me?"

"Tell you? Do you think you would've believed me? You were part right when you said I hadn't been your daddy since you were five."

There was silence as his daddy leaned forward, putting most of his weight on the front of the metal chair, his eyes wide and glaring. Alex still standing, waiting for, yet not wanting to hear what his daddy was about to say.

"It is cold out here," Alex said, "Maybe I should go?"

"No, I guess you have a right know. I do not want to take it to the grave. I did love you, and your mama until she said you were not mine."

"I don't believe you."

"And I didn't believe your mama, not a first.

But, look at the way you act. You are not one of us. I'm sorry, but I can't think of you the same way as I do my own. You are too much like her. When she left, you started pacing more, talking to yourself, screaming at Amy. She had been through enough. I had no choice but to send you away."

"You will say anything to hurt me. Who is my real daddy?"

"Hard to say? Your mother always liked preachers, she got a lot of pleasure from church, even before Rev. Tally."

Alex left him there with Amy in the house with a hall and three rooms on each side. I will feel better when I get to Levi's place.

It seemed like it had been longer than a month. Alex opened his car door to a gust of cold air. The weatherman had issued a freeze warning, first the rain and now this. He grabbed a jacket from the backseat. The sound of zipping was quick as he snugged it tight against the collar.

Alex walked to the top of the steps, it was too quiet. He paused to look toward the barn. His breath froze in the sorrow of seeing a cross out by the corn crib. Alex hurried now.

Levi was sitting in his chair by the fireplace.

"It has been a long time, Mr. Morgan."

"Almost four weeks. I'm sorry about Boo."

"Me too," Levi said, with slight tears, like Alex.

"Could you put another log on the fire? I have been cold for the last few days."

"How long have you had that cough?"

"Since last week, just after I buried Boo. She was a good dog, she died right here, beside my chair. It had been raining for a few days. We had plenty of wood on the fire. At least she was warm. I must have stayed too long in the rain. It was hard to leave her out there. I made sure she had her blanket. You know, the pink one."

"I know, she liked her blanket."

"Maybe, I better go lie down, I hate to complain. I might need a swig of cough syrup. I got some in the kitchen."

"I'm staying the weekend, If you are no better by morning, I'm going to take you to the doctor."

Levi looked older, and more than sad. Alex brought in plenty of wood, enough to last the night.

"That's the last load. I got some from the bottom of the pile. It's dry enough to burn. I'm glad the rain has slacked off some," Alex said, not knowing Levi had fallen asleep.

Alex fixed canned soup and soda crackers for supper. From the kitchen, he could hear Levi snoring. His house was smaller than he was loud. By the time Alex set the table, he had stopped.

"Levi, wake up. I got you something to eat." I hope he is all right, Levi... At last, he turned over, catching the last snore in his throat.

"I guess that cough syrup knocked me out for a while."

"You scared me," Alex said.

Levi pulled his chair up to the table. "Didn't think I was dead, did you?"

"Please don't talk like that? You know I hate the thought of anyone dying."

"The soup was good, warmed me up a bit."

"I'm glad you liked it. It is easy to cook when all you have to do is open a can. You better go back to bed, we ate kind of early, it will be dark soon. I'll keep wood on the fire."

"The rain sure sounds peaceful and gentle like upon the tin roof?" Levi said.

"You could be a poet," Alex said with a smile.

"Nah, I never could be that. I was just trying to sound like you do, sometimes. You mind getting me another blanket?"

Alex covered Levi, tucking the blanket close beneath his chin. "You are just a little tired. You wait and see, everything will be better in the morning."

"I sure miss Boo and Molly," Levi said with a soft voice. I was reading my Bible the other day, the place where it says, we will all be with the Lord one day. It didn't mention no separate place. I guess there, we will be all together. I wouldn't want to be somewhere without you.

"I got your rock, I've been saving it for you. Also, I would like you to have my Bible. One day, I hope you will write about the letter. People need to know what really happened. Alex, your mother, would have been proud of you."

"I can't hear the rain no more. Boo is barking too loud. She is there, with Molly, across the creek. Looks like a good place to fish, I'll save you a spot. We can sit on the bank and talk about old times."

Levi took Alex by the hand. "Don't be afraid, the Lord is going to take care of you.

"I just thought of something," Levi said, "You reckon there will be any raindrops in heaven?"

Levi had a gold tooth, you could only see it when he smiled.

Writing this novel was a pleasure. Please consider sharing your copy with a friend.

Perhaps you lived during that time in our history. I would love to hear from you.

TedVick.com

TED VICK

LEVI

TED VICK

CPSIA information can be obtained
at www.ICGtesting.com
Printed in the USA
BVHW032341220819
556624BV00001B/8/P